"What did you say?" He searched Melissa's face, certain she must be joking.

"We're going to have a baby." Her chin lifted with bravado, but her lower lip quivered, giving clarity to the uncertainty he'd seen in her eyes.

A thousand thoughts and emotions hit him at once.

"You're sure?"

"Yes."

"You missed a pill and didn't tell me?"

"No," she quickly replied. "Never."

"Then how?"

She glared at him before walking to the deck railing. "You're a doctor," she said without looking at him. "You tell me."

Oral contraceptive pills weren't fail-proof. Every year thousands of babies attested to that.

"But..." Damn it. He didn't want to be a father. Didn't want to risk facing what he'd gone through with Cailee. Unable to sit still, James stood and paced across the deck.

A baby. He and Melissa were going to have a baby, be parents.

Sweat covered his body. Nausea belted him in the gut. This couldn't be real.

Dear Reader,

While sneaking my mother's Mills & Boon® novels, I fell in love with romance and dreamed of a world full of hope—where good triumphs over evil, and where the girl always gets her man. Since then, I've dreamed of creating stories that touch readers' hearts.

With *The Doctor's Pregnancy Bombshell,* I've realized my dream and I can't stop grinning.

Writing a Medical Romance™ combines two of my passions: writing and nursing. Caring for patients daily gives me a fresh appreciation for life and shows me just how precious it truly is. In my fantasy world I have the ability to give everyone a fairy-tale ending—and don't we all deserve the hope of a happily-ever-after?

Like Melissa, I work in a small rural practice where everyone knows everyone. And also like Melissa, I take my patients and their problems to heart. Fortunately, I have my own real-life hero and family to keep me balanced.

I love to hear from readers. Please e-mail me at Janice@janicelynn.net, or visit me at my Web site, www.janicelynn.net.

Janice Lynn

D Keep
2-'08

THE DOCTOR'S PREGNANCY BOMBSHELL
Janice Lynn

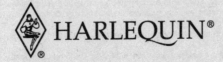

HARLEQUIN®

TORONTO • NEW YORK • LONDON
AMSTERDAM • PARIS • SYDNEY • HAMBURG
STOCKHOLM • ATHENS • TOKYO • MILAN • MADRID
PRAGUE • WARSAW • BUDAPEST • AUCKLAND

ISBN-13: 978-0-373-06634-6
ISBN-10: 0-373-06634-1

THE DOCTOR'S PREGNANCY BOMBSHELL

First North American Publication 2007

THE DOCTOR'S PREGNANCY BOMBSHELL

To Dr. Leon Reuhland for his unwavering support and guidance, for being a real-life hero to me and to his patients.

CHAPTER ONE

ONE line equals negative. Two lines equal positive.

Two lines.

Leaning against the wall of her private bathroom, Dr Melissa Conner stared in disbelief at the plastic pregnancy kit in her shaking hand. Two lines.

There had to be a mistake.

She couldn't be pregnant. Not really. Although she'd longed for a baby for as long as she could remember, she religiously took those little peach tablets meant to prevent little blue lines from multiplying. She hadn't missed a single dose.

Fighting a joy she had no right to feel under the circumstances, she grabbed the instructions. Perhaps she'd remembered the directions wrong.

Two blue lines meant negative. *For James's sake, it had to.*

The words remained the same.

She slid down the wall onto the cold tile floor with a soft thud. She'd foolishly thought stress had caused the three missed periods and frequent bathroom trips that prompted her to take a pregnancy test that morning.

Deep down she'd known the truth, but had been in denial. She was going to have a baby.

James's baby.

Her free hand went to her flat stomach. Dr James Stanley's baby grew inside her. The thought thrilled her and scared her all at the same time.

Oh, God, what would he think? He'd stressed over and over how important her birth control was, how much he didn't want children and never would.

From the time they had become involved, James had always been conscientious about contraceptive use. She hadn't minded. She'd had no more of a desire to unintentionally become a parent than James. But she had dreamed of her and James eventually marrying, having babies and the whole nine yards.

He'd quickly burst that bubble. He didn't want kids. Ever. Had explained in great, logical detail all the reasons why bringing a baby into the world would just be wrong.

Since being with James meant more than giving birth, she'd set her dreams aside and decided she'd be content to have a wonderful, caring man in her life. To distract herself from the growing longing inside her for the family she'd never had, she'd focused on another dream. Medicine.

James had continued to use a condom after they'd moved in together over a year and a half ago and had only stopped using the extra protection a few months back.

Maybe that decision had been premature.

Or the answer to her prayers that he'd change his mind about kids before her biological clock quit ticking.

"Melissa?" her nurse, Debbie, called through the

bathroom door. "You feeling OK? You've been in there a while."

Her grip on the white rectangular test kit tightened. She glanced at her watch. The hands barely read eight, but no doubt the lobby was filled with patients.

"I'm fine," she called. "Just stretching my legs."

Stretching her legs? In the bathroom? Couldn't she have thought of something more believable? Her gaze dropped to the square window with the distinct blue lines, as in plural. No, perhaps she couldn't have.

She leapt up and stuffed the test and the instructions into their box before sticking the entire kit inside the large black purse that doubled as her medical bag.

She'd deal with this later. She had patients waiting.

But, first, unable to resist, she placed her palm against her lower abdomen and smiled.

A baby. She was going to get a family after all.

Pasting on a professional mask, she opened the bathroom door and rushed past Debbie before her friend could ask questions.

Until she talked to James, she didn't have answers for her own questions, much less someone else's.

Later that morning Melissa stared out her office window at the sunshine glinting off the row of cars in the parking lot, giving everything a shiny gleam. In stark contrast to the beautiful day, her emotions were stormy.

The lump in Jamie Moss's breast wasn't merely a cyst, as hoped. The thirty-six-year-old brittle diabetic had invasive carcinoma of the left breast.

Knowing she'd delayed too long already, Melissa

turned from the window and picked up the chart off her desk.

No more delays. She was a professional and would help Jamie get through the difficult days ahead. It was only because of her already intense emotional state that she wanted to leave the office rather than give the young woman her diagnosis.

The moment she stepped into the exam room, her eyes collided with the pretty blonde's puffy ones and Melissa once again fought back tears.

Before she could speak, Jamie sniffled.

"I have cancer, don't I?" asked the shaking woman. She'd struggled to keep it together since her husband had died unexpectedly the year before of a massive heart attack.

Melissa hadn't particularly liked the man, but forty-three seemed too young to die. She dropped the chart onto the counter, sat on the stool, and took Jamie's hand.

"I'm sorry, but the tests don't look good. The radiologist says the mass I felt in your breast is cancer. I've talked with a surgeon, and he's going to see you in the morning to discuss your options. I suspect he'll recommend chemotherapy to shrink the tumor, and then he'll do a mastectomy. That means he'll remove your breast."

Jamie's arms crossed over her chest, protectively hugging her breasts.

"I can't go tomorrow." Tears streaming down her face, she shook her head in denial of much more than just the appointment date. "I don't have anyone to watch the girls."

Melissa ached at the weight of the burdens this woman carried. Jamie's hands wrenched together.

School wouldn't start again for another two weeks and she had daughters aged five and thirteen. Rarely did a week go by that Melissa didn't see either Jamie or her family. Over the years, she'd grown to think of the woman as much more than just a patient.

Last year, when Jamie's husband had died, Melissa worried her depressed friend wouldn't recover, but with help she had. Now this. Life could be so cruel.

"What about your sister? Could she go with you?" The advantage to working in a small rural practice was that she knew everything about everyone.

"She can't take time off work. She missed so much with me after Roger died that she's on probation. If she misses any more days, they'll fire her."

Melissa had no family. Until James she'd never felt connected to another person, like she belonged. If not for him, she'd be just as alone as Jamie, dealing with a totally different issue, but one just as life-changing.

What would she do if he really didn't want their baby?

"I could put her on family medical leave," Melissa offered, to keep from dwelling on her unwanted thoughts. Of course James would want their baby. Once he got used to the idea.

"I don't think that will matter." Jamie's voice sounded hollow, defeated. "But I'll let her know."

"I'll call Dr Arnold and tell him you may bring the girls with you." She squeezed her hand, wishing she could somehow give Jamie the strength she needed to get through this. "Regardless," she continued, "you need someone to go with you. You shouldn't face this alone."

"If my sister can't go, there isn't anyone," Jamie reminded her.

Sadly, Melissa knew this was the truth. Because of Jamie's mentally and emotionally abusive husband, she'd lived an isolated life prior to his death. Since then she'd struggled to make ends meet and take care of her girls. She didn't have time for making friends and her only relief from isolation consisted of trips to Melissa's, the school, the welfare office, and the grocery store for necessities.

"I'm going to call Brother Howard and see if one of the ladies from church can go with you." Melissa had called on Brother Howard a few times in the past when she'd come across a patient in dire straits. He'd never let her down. "He'll arrange for someone trustworthy to drive you to the appointment and sit with the girls while you're talking with Dr Arnold tomorrow. I can't promise anything for future visits, but I think he'll be able to help tomorrow. Would that be OK?"

Her lower lip trembling, Jamie nodded. Melissa spent another fifteen minutes with Jamie, trying to answer questions and offer assurances that Dr Arnold would do all that could be done.

The rest of Melissa's morning flew by. Mostly with seeing patients with runny noses; itchy, watery eyes; and sneezing. Living in middle Tennessee, where the pollen count soared, meant she spent a lot of time counseling on allergies and sinusitis symptoms.

"You look wiped out," Debbie commented when she walked into Melissa's office carrying two phone messages from the small local pharmacy. "Jamie seemed to take the news OK, though. She kept it together when she collected the girls." Knowing the news Melissa had had to deliver, Debbie had kept Jamie's daughters entertained in the nurses' station. "I offered to have Ramona look after the girls if she needs help."

"Is Ramona off work tomorrow?" Debbie's daughter worked at the only grocery store in town, the Piggly Wiggly, better known as "The Pig". The teenager would be starting her senior year in two short weeks.

"Yes. I gave Jamie my number. She's going to call if Brother Howard is unable to arrange someone."

Melissa nodded. One of the things she loved about Sawtooth was how people cared about each other. Having grown up in big-city foster-care, she'd missed out on the hometown warmth she now enjoyed being a part of. Actually, it could be argued that she'd missed out on warmth altogether.

"So, what gives?" Debbie dropped the messages onto Melissa's desk, then pinned her with a stare. "Besides Jamie, because I know something is bothering you. I can see it on your face."

Of course, there was also the hometown nosiness where people thought they had a right to know every minute detail of your life.

"Nothing's bothering me," she lied, knowing she needed to talk with James before anyone else. "Just a little tired."

"Yummy Dr James keeping you up too late?"

Hardly.

He'd been working more and more lately. She hadn't complained. It was easier to hide how nauseous she was when they only spent a few hours together here and there. Because she had been hiding her symptoms. From James and from herself. Facing them meant facing decisions she didn't want to make. Like what she'd do if the most important person in her life didn't change his mind about wanting a baby.

"He worked the emergency room shift at Vanderbilt last night and had late meetings the night before. I've not seen him for a couple of days." Not wanting to go into more details, she picked up her messages, skimming their content. One was a routine medication refill request, the other a newer patient who Melissa suspected of being a drug seeker.

Debbie's eyes narrowed. "Are you and Super Doctor getting along OK?"

"We're fine." Except James didn't want kids and, according to the two blue lines, he was going to be a daddy. She closed her eyes, envisioning a little boy with James's dimples or a little girl with his dark hair and blue eyes. A baby. Her heart squeezed.

Memories of them volunteering at Vanderbilt Children's Hospital last Christmas played through her mind. The children had swarmed all over James while he'd entertained them with corny jokes and silly magic tricks that Melissa still hadn't quite figured out. She'd laughed so hard at him that her eyes had watered. Only now, with the clarity of hindsight, did she see that those tears had been much more. She'd wanted that. James playing with children. Their children. That night they'd argued, but James had refused to budge on his views. No kids. She'd told herself it was OK that he didn't want children, that just having him was enough.

If James persisted in not wanting their child, she'd have to learn to accept it. Regardless, she wouldn't ever let her baby have to deal with the feelings of being uncared for that Melissa herself had faced as a child.

"Stretching again?"

Melissa blinked. "What?"

Tucking a short strand of chestnut hair behind an ear, Debbie cocked her hip against the desk. "Thought you might be stretching your eyes the way you were stretching those long legs this morning."

Not meeting her friend's eyes, she shuffled through some papers on her desk. "Like I said, I'm just tired."

Debbie shook her head and sighed. "OK, but when you're ready to talk, know I'm here for you."

Dr James Stanley turned his Mustang into the driveway of the house he shared with Melissa. God, he was tired of this drive.

Between his two twenty-four-hour shifts a week in Vanderbilt's emergency room, his research, and his teaching stint for the university, he kept a full slate in Nashville. Living an hour away was damned inconvenient, but he couldn't convince Melissa to transfer from her small-town practice.

Life would be much simpler if she'd agree to take a job with the university like he wanted.

Sometimes he thought he'd made life too easy by moving in with her. Had he stayed in Nashville, perhaps she'd have seen the advantages of living in the city.

Instead, she'd hinted that she'd like him to join her practice—like he wanted to do pap smears and tonsil checks all day.

No, he liked the grittiness of working in a major trauma hospital. An emergency room to where the worst of the worst were airlifted. He liked the challenge of taking a broken body and putting it back together. Like today, he'd worked two code blues and revived both flatline victims. He lived to stare death in the face and snatch a person back from its greedy grip.

He couldn't get that in a Podunk, Sawtooth, family practice that was already sucking all Melissa's energy, not to mention her time.

He missed her. The way she looked at him when she wanted his attention but didn't want to interrupt whatever he was doing. The way she sang to herself in the shower when she thought he couldn't hear. The way her eyes lit up when their gazes met and he'd wink, letting her know how special she was. The way she melted in his arms when they touched. He missed everything about her.

Rarely did they spend an uninterrupted evening together these days. The phone would ring and Melissa always took the calls. Always rushed to whoever's rescue. Some nights he never saw her, which made the time he spent on the road useless.

More and more he opted to sleep over at a friend's apartment when he became engrossed in his research and time slipped away. But once he was home, he was home.

That's what he liked about the emergency room. He patched 'em up and moved on to the next cubicle.

Melissa thought she was supposed to be on twenty-four seven call to her patients' every whim.

James gripped the steering wheel, wondering why he was getting so worked up. Probably just fatigue. Thirty-six hours with no sleep would do that to a man.

A hot shower, a decent meal, and Melissa, and he'd be good for a few hours before crashing.

Only when he clicked the garage door open, the bay sat empty. No Jeep Cherokee. James sighed, reminding himself exhaustion caused his annoyance.

Had he known he was coming home to an empty house, he would have stayed late with Kristen to review a course syllabus for next semester. She'd taken over an EKG class for a cardiologist who'd retired over the summer and wanted James's input. He smiled at the thought of the pretty young doctor being so nervous of facing the incoming students. He remembered being just as anxious about his first teaching stint.

He liked Kristen. She was a lot like him. Loved medicine, but still found time to love life, too.

Once upon a time, Melissa had loved life. Memories invaded of them picnicking at Centennial Park. An unexpected spring shower had drenched them. They'd laughed, gathered their things, and, hand in hand and half-oblivious to the raindrops pelting them, had walked back to his apartment. They'd made love for the first time that afternoon. Holding her afterwards, he'd known Melissa was unlike any woman he'd ever known, that she meant more to him than any sane man would ever admit. She still meant that much.

But she'd changed, become engrossed in her work to

the point she was only a shadow of the woman he'd fallen for.

Was she unhappy in their relationship? Was that why she'd gone from the dedicated but vibrant woman of two years ago to the workaholic he now lived with?

A shower, salad, and grilled steak later, James nursed a beer while reclining on a lounge chair on the long wooden deck that ran the back length of the house. The sun dipped behind the wooded hills, streaking the sky with hues of pink and orange. Birds chirped in the distance and two squirrels chased each other up a tree. A light breeze broke the heat, ruffling his hair. He could appreciate what Melissa saw in this place where the Tennessee Hills met the Appalachian Mountains, but he preferred the hum of the city.

That's when he realized just how dissatisfied he'd grown with his and Melissa's relationship. It seemed to him that he was the one making all the concessions so they could spend time together. On the occasions he arranged time off at the weekends, she had no problem ditching him to see this patient or that.

He admired her dedication, but needed more from the woman in his life than she was giving.

Was it time to cut their ties?

He couldn't imagine his life without her but, then, she really wasn't in his life these days. Even their once amazing sex life had fizzled out over the past couple of months to tired gropes in the middle of the night.

But those tired gropes appealed more than wild sex with any other woman.

Which was why he'd been in his relationship with

Melissa longer than any other. They'd been together two years that had been in some ways the best of his life, particularly in the beginning when they hadn't been able to get enough of each other's company or bodies.

But he and Melissa needed a shake-up.

He was tired of coming last, and if something didn't change soon he would move on.

The buzz of the garage door opening warned she had finally come home. He glanced at his watch. After eight-thirty.

A couple of minutes later the screen door screeched. He didn't turn, just kept watching the squirrels playing in the fading sunlight.

He smelled the soft vanilla that always clung to her skin before she stepped into his line of vision. She came up beside him and kissed his forehead.

"Hey," she said, dropping into the wrought-iron chair next to his, the floral cushion squishing beneath her.

Was it wrong that he wanted her to value their time together? Plain and simple, she took him for granted.

The more he thought about it, moving back to Nashville might be just what the doctor ordered.

"James?"

He bit his tongue to keep from responding.

"Is something wrong?"

He sighed. He was being such a jerk. She'd been out working, not screwing around.

"Just tired." He turned toward her and frowned.

She looked awful.

Or at least as awful as a woman with Melissa's classic features could look. Dark circles marred the pale skin beneath her almond-shaped eyes, and wisps of honey-colored hair haphazardly escaped the tight ponytail she usually wore.

"There's steak and salad on the kitchen counter." No need of her passing out from hypoglycemia when he told her he was moving. Let her eat, get her blood sugar up, and then he'd drop his bombshell. He'd remind her that he wasn't content to be constantly shoved aside.

She wrinkled her nose. "I'm not hungry."

"You need to eat. You've lost weight."

The skin over her cheeks was taut and the fullness of her curves had lost their lushness. She looked gaunt. She worked too hard, probably forgot to eat altogether when her office was busy, which was most of the time.

"Rough day?" she asked, averting her gaze at his continued scrutiny.

His frown deepened, but he let her change the topic of conversation as she looked ready to collapse.

"Not particularly. No one died." Nobody dying always made for a better day when one worked in the medical profession. "At least, no one I wasn't able to bring back."

Death, the opponent he faced daily.

"That's good." She stared off into the woods, her astute eyes quickly picking out a deer grazing at the border of the trees. But she was on edge. Totally un-Melissa-like.

"Something happen?" he asked.

She blew out a long breath. "Ray Barnes got caught in his combine."

He winced. Having worked on farming-equipment cases, he knew the man would have been a mess.

Although he would have gotten an adrenaline rush from taking care of such a patient, Melissa preferred the routine aspects of medicine that bored him senseless.

"There wasn't anything I could do." Her voice trembled. "He died before he could be airlifted to Nashville." She closed her eyes. "I've been with Wilma and their daughters all evening."

The image of a portly white-haired woman and two spinsters in their forties came to mind.

Melissa's shoulders shook, but she didn't make a sound. Only the singing of crickets broke the silence.

James could feel her pain and struggled to find the right words to give her comfort. How was it he could calm a dying woman while he put life back into her body, but felt useless when it came to Melissa?

"How's she holding up?" he finally asked, breaking the silence.

"Not well." Her eyes remained shut. "At her daughters' request, I prescribed Valium to help her rest." A soft hiccup jerked at his heart. How could he dump his unhappiness with their relationship on her when she'd had such an awful day?

"I promised Lila and Faye I'd stop by to check on her in the morning before I go in to the office," she continued.

And there was his answer.

There would always be some patient with a problem that Melissa took on as her own standing between them, taking precedence over anything they shared.

No doubt she'd made house calls that morning before starting her day at the office, too.

"You should have her come into the clinic like

everyone else." Only everyone else didn't come into the office. They expected Melissa to run to them. Just look at what it was doing to her. "You can't keep spoiling these people."

Melissa's eyes opened. "Taking good care of my patients isn't spoiling them. Besides, say what you will, but I've seen you in action." A weary smile played on her lips. "Few doctors can rival your bedside manner."

"My patients don't think its OK to invade my personal time." His words weren't anything he hadn't said a hundred times before, but tonight each one seemed to penetrate Melissa.

"What would you have me do? Tell Wilma to grow up? That death is a part of life and to just deal with it?" Anger pierced her questions. "The woman found her husband crushed, cut to pieces, held him while he died. Give her a break if she was half-hysterical with grief and I refused to leave her until I knew she was going to be OK."

Death was a part of life and a person did just have to deal with it.

James knew that better than anyone. He did his damnedest every day to cheat death, and still memories of the lives he had failed to save haunted him. Cailee, his baby sister, in particular. Oh, yeah, death was a part of life, and he had dealt with it, but that didn't mean he ever saw a baby without remembering the three-month-old sister he hadn't been able to save.

Closing his mind to the past, he took a sip of his lukewarm beer. "You're right. I'm just frustrated that yet again we missed out on spending the evening together."

He patted his lounge chair, indicating he wanted her to sit with him.

Melissa's anger evaporated as quickly as it had appeared and she settled between his legs, her back pressed against his chest.

He wrapped his arms around her, breathing in her warm fragrance, wishing he could snap back to the beginning when she'd rushed home to him every night, when he'd been able to look at her and know he put the glow on her face.

She snuggled closer. God, she'd lost more weight than he'd realized. He'd only stayed in Nashville for two nights. Hadn't she eaten while he'd been gone?

He removed the band holding her hair and dropped it onto the deck. Her hair cascaded around her shoulders like a silky curtain. James inhaled the scent of her shampoo. His body stirred against her bottom pressed enticingly into the V of his legs.

She placed her hands over his and squeezed. "I'm sorry I wasn't home when you got here," she softly apologized.

"Me, too." Because it was the catalyst that had pushed him into making a hard decision.

If he wanted the magic back, he had to make it happen.

She relaxed against him, running her palms over his denim-covered thighs in a caress. "This is nice."

It was nice. And long overdue. Too much work and too little time was hard on any relationship. Theirs was no exception. He needed to pressure her to quit this country craziness and relocate to a job that wouldn't demand so much from her soul.

"I'm moving out tomorrow."

CHAPTER TWO

MELISSA stiffened, her life flashing before her much as she imagined it did prior to death. She had to have heard wrong. She twisted and their gazes met in the failing light.

"What did you say?"

James's eyes appeared almost midnight-black, but they held steady. "I'm moving to Nashville."

The words pelted her heart like chunks of hail through rusty tin. He was leaving?

Shocked, hurt, *reeling*, she scooted out of his embrace. How could he hold her and tell her he was dumping her in the same breath?

He couldn't be dumping her.

"You're breaking up with me?" The question sounded so high schoolish, but she didn't know how else to take his words.

"I think we need some space apart."

Space needed. The kiss of death for any relationship.

"You've met someone, haven't you?" She ached at the thought, but why else would he suddenly decide to move out?

"That isn't it."

"Then what is?"

"Us."

"Us? What's wrong with us?"

"Just about everything."

Melissa gasped. She couldn't help it. How could she have missed that James was so unhappy?

Then again, maybe this was why he'd been spending more and more nights in Nashville. She should have seen the end coming. Didn't she know better than to think anyone would stick around for her?

"What's her name?"

James wasn't the type of man not to have a woman in his life. Now that she thought of it, they hadn't had much of a life together for some time. *How had that happened?*

"This is ridiculous, Melissa. I say I'm moving out and you automatically assume I'm involved with someone. Do you really think I'd do that? Become involved with someone while living with you?"

Was he moving so he could become involved with whoever it was he'd met? She thought over the names she'd heard him mention over the past few months. Only one stood out.

"It's Dr Weaver, isn't it?" She held back a sob at the thought of the pretty cardiologist James had introduced her to at the last meeting she'd attended with him. The brunette had been the guest speaker, discussing the impact of angiotensin receptor blockers on the long-term outcomes of patients with hypertension. Melissa had gotten tingles of unease at the way the woman had watched James, but when she'd asked him about it, he'd laughed away her concerns. Now who was laughing? Certainly not her.

"Kristen?" He frowned, seeming surprised that she had put one and one together so quickly. His mouth opened to deny her accusation, but he must have decided the truth would eventually come out. "Kristen and I work together on a research project at the hospital and as university faculty colleagues. She's a beautiful, intelligent woman."

And she'd acted half in love with James at that meeting. Apparently Melissa's suspicions hadn't been so unfounded after all.

"I hope you'll be happy together." A lie. Petty of her, but she didn't want some other woman making James happy.

A snortlike sound erupted from deep within his chest. "That's it? I tell you we need space and you toss me to another woman and say you hope we'll be happy together?"

"What do you want me to say?"

"The truth."

The truth. She wasn't sure he could handle the truth.

She bit the inside of her lip, making fast decisions and probably coming up with all the wrong answers.

"Fine. You want the truth. I'll give it to you." But she hesitated, wondering if she should just keep her mouth shut. If he was leaving, did she really want to tell him? She didn't. But, ethically, now that she knew for certain, could she keep her pregnancy from him, even if only for a short while? Wouldn't it be better to just get it all out in the open up front?

"I'm listening," James reminded her when she still hesitated.

"I'm not sure how to say this, except you need to know before we go further with this conversation." Her eyes lifted to his and she prayed he'd somehow see into her heart and tell her what she needed to hear him say. "I'm pregnant."

For the first time in his life James wondered if he might be having a panic attack.

Either that or he was having a heart attack.

He preferred to think the pain in his chest resulted from severe anxiety as he was a fairly fit thirty-three-year-old and had no family history of heart problems.

"What did you say?" He searched Melissa's face, certain she must be joking, although he didn't find her comment the slightest bit funny.

"We're going to have a baby." Her chin lifted with bravado, but her lower lip quivered, giving clarity to the uncertainty he'd seen in her eyes.

A thousand thoughts and emotions hit him at once.

"You're sure?"

"Yes."

"You missed a Pill and didn't tell me?"

"No," she quickly denied. "Never."

"Then how?"

She glared at him before walking to the deck railing. Her knuckles whitened against the handrail. She stared out at the hills she claimed to love so much.

"You're a doctor," she said, without looking at him. "You tell me."

Oral contraceptive pills weren't failproof. Every year thousands of babies attested to that.

"But…" Damn it. He didn't want to be a statistic. He didn't want to be a father. Didn't want Melissa pregnant, didn't want a baby, to risk facing what he'd gone through with Cailee, what he'd watched his parents go through prior to their divorce. "I knew I shouldn't have quit using condoms."

Melissa spun, pinning him with a scowl. "Don't you dare blame me for that. You made that decision all on your own."

True. Melissa had been on the Pill the entire year and a half they'd lived together. He'd forgotten to buy condoms. When he'd woken up needing her, and her warm body had actually been curled next to him, he'd decided, Why not? Being inside her with nothing between them—their first skin-to-skin experience— had been amazing. He'd felt reconnected to her, like they'd recaptured the closeness from those first few months. From that point on, they hadn't used extra protection.

"I'm not blaming anyone." Except himself for putting her in this position. Of putting himself in this position. A baby? He couldn't do it.

"Sure sounded that way." Accusation and hurt coated her words.

James raked his fingers through his hair. This couldn't be happening. "Look, you know how I feel."

Not all the reasons why, but he'd not beat around the bush. Point-blank he'd told her that he never wanted children and she'd agreed.

"I didn't do this by myself and sure didn't plan for it to happen."

"I'm not saying you did." Everything he said was coming out wrong. He didn't want to hurt Melissa. He wanted to do and say things to comfort her, to take the horrified look off her face, but he didn't want a baby. "I'm trying to figure out what to do about it."

"It? As in our baby *it*?" Her eyes narrowed and her voice bubbled on the verge of hysteria. "We aren't doing anything about our baby, so just put that thought out of your head."

Do anything? She thought…

"I wasn't insinuating you should have an abortion, Melissa. That didn't even cross my mind." Wouldn't cross his mind. He'd sworn to protect lives the day he'd taken his doctor's oath and, for him, that meant at every stage.

"Weren't you?" she accused. Her entire body shook and as the temperature was in the balmy high seventies, it couldn't be from cold.

Unable to sit still, James stood, paced across the deck. A baby. He and Melissa were going to have a baby, be parents.

Sweat covered his body. Nausea belted him in the gut. Any moment he expected the earth to open up and swallow him. This couldn't be real.

"When?"

"I'm not sure. I took the test this morning."

"Why?"

"I missed my period. Actually…" Her head lowered and, although he couldn't see her face, he knew she'd closed her eyes "…I've missed three."

Three? Dear Lord, she would be over three months pregnant.

"Why did you wait so long to check?"

Her tongue darted out, moistening her lips. "At first I thought I might have a touch of a stomach virus. It's not uncommon to temporarily lose your period when you've lost weight." She shrugged. "I guess I was in denial, too. I kept thinking I couldn't really be."

Other than her thinness, he hadn't noticed her symptoms. Then again, it had been weeks since they'd sat down to a meal together or spent more than a few passing minutes in each other's company. It was like she'd been avoiding him. A baby. Maybe she had.

His vision dimmed and he clutched his forehead. Visions of Cailee snapped in front of his eyes, taunting him, his future. She'd have been seventeen now. The same age he had been when she'd died.

"I can't do this."

She gave him an appalled look. "What do you mean, 'do this'?"

"Have a baby."

She whimpered, a half pained, half strangled cry. "I guess it's a good thing you don't have to do anything."

James winced, feeling her hurt and anger but too overwhelmed with his own emotions to address hers.

"This can't be happening."

"Just what every woman wants to hear when she tells a man he's going to be a dad."

"I don't want to be a dad," he reminded her. "I've never deceived you. No babies ever. You knew that. You agreed."

"No one is going to make you be a dad."

"You said you wouldn't—"

"No, I wouldn't, but biologically I can't change my baby's genetics. But that doesn't mean you have to do a thing, James. Not one blasted thing." She shuddered. "Move to Nashville. I don't need you."

She didn't need him. Or anyone else. Not normally. But looking at the anguish on her face, he suspected she needed more than she wanted to admit.

Which made his chest hurt more.

"I'm not going to leave you." Hell, he'd never wanted to leave her to begin with. Not really. He'd just wanted her to see what she was doing to their relationship, for her to put some effort in, too. "Not like this."

"I don't want you to stay *like this*. Go and be with Kristen or whatever appeals so much about Nashville."

He stared at her in disbelief. She thought he would walk away from a woman he'd made pregnant? Did she know him so little? And how would he ever convince her that his decision to move out had stemmed from wanting *her* to notice him, not some other woman?

Then again, his reaction hadn't exactly been ecstatic and he didn't blame her for her hurt expression.

His timing had been way off. As usual. Which was why he'd avoided relationships. Until Melissa. One look and he'd been hooked. Before he'd known it he'd wanted nothing more than to spend all his free time with her.

A whimper had his attention shooting back to her. She'd turned away from him to stare out into the night, her back straight. Too straight.

She was crying, but trying to hold it in. He started to reach for her, to wrap his arms around her, and tell her that somehow all this would be OK. He cared for her and they'd work through this. Her cell phone rang, so he cursed instead.

"Don't answer," he ordered when she reached for the phone clipped to her waistband.

Pulling herself together, she swiped at her eyes. "It might be a patient."

"Which is why you shouldn't answer. For once, make me your priority."

"I can't not answer. It might be an emergency." She ignored his plea, removed her phone, and flipped it open. "Dr Conner speaking."

James seethed. How could she answer the phone during such a significant personal conversation? Would he always rate so far beneath the needs of her patients?

What of her pregnancy? How would she take care of a baby when she couldn't even take care of herself because of the demands Sawtooth placed upon her?

Her face paler than ever, she closed the phone.

"I've got to go." Big surprise. "Mrs Barnes over-dosed on the Valium I gave her. She's being rushed by ambulance to Dekalb General."

She started walking toward the door, but he grabbed her arm, struck again by its leanness.

"Fine," he ground out. "Let the paramedics and the ER doctor do their job. You don't have to be there."

"She's my patient."

"You're off duty. There are others who can take care of her."

She stared at him a moment, then jerked her arm free. "That's where you're wrong. When it comes to people I care about, I'm never off duty."

Which slapped him right at the heart of the matter. Just how much did she care for him? Because she never seemed "on duty" when it came to their relationship.

"Don't go."

She paused, her hand on the screen door handle.

"I need you here," he admitted. "We need to finish our discussion."

Her chest expanded, then fell. "I'll be back in a few hours. We'll talk then."

With that, she left.

Rage filled James. How could she walk away in the middle of a conversation about their future?

Because her future was here, in Sawtooth, where everybody knew everybody and you couldn't turn around without someone knowing what you were doing.

The barely visible view from the deck no longer impressed him. Now the dimness only offered a bleakness he refused to bear.

No way was he going to sit in this house alone tonight while she left him.

Melissa grabbed her black bag off the kitchen counter where she'd set it when she'd come home. Her gaze landed on the steak and salad fixings James had left out for her. Her stomach churned.

He was leaving.

Had she somehow known this was coming when she'd ignored her symptoms week after week? When she'd confirmed her pregnancy? Had she known that she would lose James?

He hadn't taken her news well.

Had she really expected him to? Apparently she had. Deep inside, she'd thought he'd warm to the idea. That, really, James liked kids, would make a wonderful father. She'd known he would need to get over the initial shock, but she'd hoped, expected he'd realize what a blessing her pregnancy was.

But he'd told her he was moving out *before* she'd told him her news.

It wasn't the baby driving him away. It was her.

Her legs threatened to buckle. James would be packing his things and leaving. No more nights of lying in his arms. No more mornings of waking up with the pillow next to her imprinted with him. No more breathing in his musky scent. No more James.

She leaned her head against the refrigerator. She didn't have time to dwell on this. Not right now.

Wilma Barnes and her daughters needed her.

She got her keys out and on the way to her car hit the garage door button. The door immediately ground open.

Despite knowing she had to go, her heart and body protested. She needed rest. And James.

Truth be told, she wouldn't be sleeping even if she had stayed at home. Not with visions of his reaction playing in her head. Did he plan to stay the night? Have one for old time's sake and then leave tomorrow? Or would he be gone when she got home?

Fighting tears and hating her hormonal state, she stuck her key in the ignition and started her car.

Her car door opened, causing her to jump.

"Move over. I'm driving."

She gawked at James.

"Mrs Barnes is my patient. I can handle her."

Not to mention that James never had anything to do with her patients.

"You're too tired to drive to Dekalb, much less face a suicidal woman and her family. Move over."

The stubborn set to his clean-shaven jaw said he wasn't going to budge and unless she wanted to risk reversing over him, she'd have to scoot. She ought to put the vehicle in reverse and accelerate. Would serve him right.

But she couldn't deny what he'd said. She was tired. Bone-weary tired, and the thought of resting for the twenty-minute drive tempted her too much to argue. She crossed over into the passenger seat and closed her eyes. Just a quick rest, then she'd feel like facing James.

Melissa woke with a start.

Immediately, her gaze went to the digital clock on the dashboard. Not lit. Because the car wasn't running. Because there wasn't a driver. Because the car was parked in the small gated physicians' lot at Dekalb General.

Where was James and why hadn't he woken her up when they'd arrived?

She opened the locked door and shifted her wrist to where the overhead light illuminated her watch. Almost eleven.

She must have been more tired than she'd thought.

Stretching, she eased from the car and rubbed her

lower back. Upon standing, dizziness hit her and she grabbed hold of the roof.

Her stomach growled, reminding her of what ailed her. Because of the nausea, she hadn't managed more than a few crackers all day. And not much more than that the day before.

Digging through her black bag, she found a pack of breath fresheners and tossed a couple in her mouth. At least her mouth would be minty clean. She locked the car and headed into the hospital.

What she saw in the waiting room surprised her.

James sat holding Lila Barnes's hand. The woman's nose glowed a bright red and her face was swollen from tears. She looked adoringly at James. No wonder, he was handsome as sin and oozed charm. The woman didn't know him well enough to notice the way he held his jaw, the slow foot tap, the determined gleam in his eyes. What Lila saw was a charming doctor who listened attentively.

What Melissa saw was a man shrouded by protective walls because he refused to become attached. He comforted, but only on the surface, only when it didn't require exposing himself.

Why hadn't she noticed that about him before? How he kept himself closed off from his patients? Was it because of the confidence he exuded in his skills? Now she saw the truth.

James refused to open up and care about his patients as anything other than patients. He didn't see them as people with real lives and families, just as the heart attack in bay one or the motor vehicle accident in bay two.

James kept himself closed off from her, too, but distracted her with his charm and sexual finesse. He kept her on the outside of that wall, just as he locked out the rest of the world.

When Lila and James looked up, Melissa, not willing to discuss private matters with James in front of the woman or in the middle of a hospital waiting room, offered a weak smile. "You should have woken me up when we got here."

He stood, brushing his hand over his loose jeans that still managed to showcase his lean hips and thighs to perfection. Mercy. No wonder she stayed distracted.

"There was nothing I couldn't handle."

Except giving Lila his real concern. Or her.

Although he gave her his body, which she greedily took, he'd never given her a glimpse of his heart.

Unable to stop the stab of pain in her chest and not wanting James to see her disillusionment, she turned to Wilma's daughter. "How's your mom?"

The round-faced woman drew in a deep breath, before sending another doting glance at James. "Dr Stanley just came from checking on her and he says she's going to be OK."

"Checking her?" What happened to letting the paramedics and ER doctor handle it?

James's face revealed nothing. "Dr Kirby is the staff doctor tonight. As I was here, he thought I should give her a once-over. She'll recover fully."

James had willingly seen one of her patients. Why? What kind of game was he playing?

She plopped into the closest chair.

"Poor thing. She's dead on her feet," Lila cooed in a motherly fashion, despite the fact that she was only a few years older than Melissa. Neither did the fact that Melissa was there stop them from discussing her as if she wasn't.

"I agree." James addressed Lila, but his eyes never left Melissa. She could feel them boring into her, like he knew she'd discovered his secret—that he hid behind walls. "I've talked with Dr Kirby. He's going to arrange for a cot to be placed in whatever room your mother is assigned to on the medical floor. You and your sister can stay the night with her if you like."

The woman praised James, making Melissa's nausea worse.

"Now," Lila ordered, sending a concerned look Melissa's way, "get Dr Conner home for some rest."

James planned to do just that.

He'd thought she'd appeared tired earlier in the evening and he'd not known the cause. Now he knew. Melissa was pregnant and that explained the fatigue etched on her face.

He felt stupid for not picking up on the signs, but for months they'd been leading separate lives, with the occasional late evening spent together and nighttime sex thrown in.

Now they were going to be parents.

James took Melissa's hand, ignored the tingle of awareness that always came with touching her, and helped her to her feet. He placed a guiding hand in the small of her back.

"I'm fine," she protested. "Just tired."

Which was his line from earlier, when he hadn't been fine at all but contemplating shaking up her world so she'd notice him. If he'd only known.

Not that he hadn't been tired, too. He'd been without sleep more hours than he cared to consider. But he'd spoken out of frustration. Frustration he still felt.

How were they going to bring a baby into the world and provide a happy home when Melissa valued his presence in her life so little? When a baby was the last thing he wanted and the one thing in life he feared most?

He assisted a tight-lipped Melissa into her car and was ten minutes into the drive before he glanced toward her. Her eyes were closed, but she wasn't asleep.

She looked vulnerable. Which made him want to go and slay dragons on her behalf. Crazy. Melissa preferred slaying her own dragons.

But she didn't look capable of swatting away a kitten, much less slaying a dragon.

"We're getting married." James wasn't quite sure where the comment had come from and it couldn't have surprised Melissa any more than it had him.

Her eyes opened and she rolled her head toward him. "Married?"

"As soon as it can be arranged. My parents will want to fly in from Boston." Now that the idea had formed, his mind raced ahead. Whether he'd meant to become a father or not, Melissa was pregnant with his baby and he took his responsibilities seriously. A baby changed everything. She'd have to make concessions whether she wanted to or not. "You can start looking for someone to buy your practice."

"Buy my practice?" Her head jerked up. "I'm not selling my practice."

James shot a quick look at her then returned his gaze to the road. "You'll want to stay home after the baby arrives."

"No, I won't." She shook her head.

She wanted to keep practicing? What was he saying? This was Melissa. Of course she'd want to keep practicing. Medicine was in her blood, but her practice took too much of her time.

"I can get you on at the hospital. We'll hire a nanny to help with the baby." They'd make it work. And he'd somehow deal with his worst fear, having a baby. "Two weeks? Maybe three? However long it takes to apply for a license and throw a quick ceremony together. We can be married within a month."

"Earlier tonight you were moving out of my house so you could be with another woman." Melissa squinted at him. "Now you're proposing?"

CHAPTER THREE

THE next morning Melissa went through the motions of her day, wondering how she could fault James for being detached when she was so removed from everything.

Removed? No, that wasn't the right word. Overwhelmed was more like it.

"If you don't tell me what's going on, I'm going to scream." Debbie shut Melissa's office door and leaned against it. "I've tried to ignore your ghastly appearance in the hope you'll tell me, but you just keep holding it in. And don't even think for a minute that I didn't hear you being sick this morning."

Melissa touched her face. Did she look that bad? She couldn't remember doing more that morning than brushing her teeth. Perhaps she should have taken time for makeup, but she'd wanted to go to Dekalb General before coming in to the office.

James had been sitting at the kitchen bar, working on a glass of orange juice and reviewing a stack of papers, probably things to do with the new school semester. He'd watched her pour a glass of juice and force her way through it and a piece of toast.

"Will you be here tonight?" she'd asked.

"Yes. We need to talk." He'd insisted she go to bed when they'd gotten home the night before and, for the first time ever, he'd slept in the guest room. "If our relationship means anything to you, you'll prove it by coming home so we can spend the evening discussing our future. Can you be here by six?"

Knowing he was right, that they had many things to work out between them, she'd nodded.

"Hello." Debbie snapped her fingers in front of Melissa's face. "Earth to Dr Melissa Conner."

Melissa blinked. "Sorry."

Debbie crossed her arms. "I'm not letting you out of this office until you tell me what gives."

"I'm pregnant."

Debbie smiled in an I-knew-it sort of way. She clasped her hands together and wiggled excitedly. "Omigosh. This is fabulous. What does James say?"

Melissa sighed, knowing she couldn't keep this bottled inside her any longer. She needed to talk and Debbie was her best friend. "Right before I broke the news he announced he's moving to Nashville."

"No way." Debbie looked appropriately stunned, then outraged. "The jerk."

Melissa shrugged, not wanting her friend to think unkindly of James. "He didn't know I was pregnant when he told me."

"Now that he knows?"

"He mentioned marriage, but I don't know." Maybe before he'd stated his intention to move she might have considered it. Now she only felt like she was forcing him into yet something else he didn't want. She didn't want to spend the rest of her life with a man who didn't want to be with her and their baby. A man who, on the surface, would do and say all the right things but he'd never let her touch the real him.

A man who would insist she give up a career she loved, just as he'd once insisted she give up her dream of a baby or give him up.

Debbie sank into the chair next to Melissa's desk. "I can understand that. It would be hard to accept a proposal from someone who was planning to leave you until he found out you were pregnant."

"Exactly." Melissa closed her eyes. "I think he's met someone else."

"You're kidding!"

"I wish." Melissa rolled her neck, trying to ease the tightness gripping her muscles. "I met her once. Tall, gorgeous, brunette. Think supermodel with a stethoscope and a penchant for hearts."

Debbie shook her head. "James isn't the kind of man to be taken in by just looks."

"She's a cardiologist at Vanderbilt. She and James share a research grant on the prevention of damage to the heart during myocardial infarctions by administering certain types of medications. He thinks she's brilliant."

Wincing, Debbie mouthed an O. "So, what are you going to do about this woman?"

"I'm not sure."

"Fight for him." Debbie's face took on a thoughtful expression. "I've seen how James looks at you. Despite whatever problems you are having, the man loves you. You're carrying his baby. And at the moment he sleeps in your bed. You have the advantage, Melissa. Take it."

"He's never told me he loves me."

"Doesn't make it any less true," Debbie pointed out. "Have you told him?"

"No." She hadn't really thought about how she felt about James. He was a part of her life. A good part, even if he did keep so much of himself locked away. She cared for him, wanted him in her life, but love?

Loving someone was just begging to be hurt.

"You do love James, don't you?" Debbie's question echoed her thoughts.

Definitely Melissa was closer to him than any other person who'd ever come into her life. She couldn't imagine her life without him in it, but was that love?

"You're thinking about this way too long."

"I care for him." Melissa opted for a safe answer, not wanting her friend to know how much it hurt that James might leave.

"That's a lame answer." Her friend didn't mince her words. "I was feeling sorry for you, but maybe it's James who deserves my sympathy. You've been seeing him for two years and you don't know if you love him?"

Melissa grimaced.

"Well, let me point out the obvious. You're crazy about James and if you lose him because you're too afraid to admit it, then it's no one's fault but your own."

"He's the one who holds his emotions in. Not me."

"Oh, really?" Debbie's brow quirked. "I'd say you've got one heck of a fortress around your heart. If you want to keep James in your life, you're going to have to open the door and let him in."

"You have it all wrong," Melissa said defensively. "He's the one with the fortress. He won't let me in."

"OK, let's just say you both have issues. But one of you is going to have to take a chance and let the other in. You have a baby to think about. What are you going to say to him or her? That you and James didn't make it because you weren't willing to trust each other with your feelings?"

Debbie made her fears seem petty, but how did one say, "I want you to let me in"?

"Look, you don't have anything major on your schedule this afternoon. Let me see what I can reschedule until tomorrow, the rest I'll have come in early. Go, get your hair and makeup done, because you've had better days." Definitely no mincing of words. "Buy new underwear." Debbie thought new underwear solved every problem. "Tell James how you feel about him and your relationship. See what happens. The heart doctor doesn't stand a chance. Not if you're willing to make James your priority."

Hadn't James said something to the effect of making him her priority? Was she more to blame for the problems they faced than she'd realized?

Granted, she hadn't been the one to announce she was leaving, but part of her fear of pregnancy originated because deep down she knew her relationship with James wasn't what it should be. Hadn't been for months. Was that why she'd delayed taking her pregnancy test for so long? Had it been easier to ignore her symptoms, ignore him, than to face the realities of her life?

It had been too easy to put off their plans when something had come up. After all, she'd see him whenever she got home. Only more and more he hadn't been home. He'd been in Nashville. With Dr Kristen Weaver, who jumped every time James had glanced her way and had her priorities straight.

Melissa grimaced. She'd taken James's presence in her life for granted. No wonder he hadn't let her behind those walls.

She didn't want to lose him.

During the early part of their relationship, she'd been happy. Because of him, the way he'd made her feel about herself, the way she'd felt about him.

"OK," she agreed, knowing she couldn't let him walk out of her life without knowing she wanted him to stay. "See what you can reschedule. Call Peggy Williams." She named one of her patients who owned a beauty salon and was forever offering her services. "See if she can give me the works."

For the rest of the afternoon, Melissa stayed focused on her patients. Mrs Erma Johnson needed a refill on her blood pressure medicine. Darla Qualls had an allergic reaction to her antibiotic. Melissa glanced at her last chart of the day. Samantha Cantor, a pretty teenager who would soon be starting university about half an hour's drive away.

"Hi, Sam," she said, entering the exam room and glancing at Debbie's notation on the chart. Pain with urination for two weeks. "Are you burning when you go to the bathroom?"

"Some, but my stomach hurts all the time." She rubbed

her suprapubic area, the lowest part of the abdomen, which rested above her pubic bone. "Right here."

"Have you noticed a strong odor or seen any blood?"

Sam nodded. "This is a bit embarrassing, but sex hurts. I have a horrible discharge. It's…" her face turned bright red "…green and foamy."

Sounded like *Trichomonas pallidium*. "How many sexual partners have you had?"

Sam's cheeks glowed. "Just one. Bobby and I have been dating for three years. Nothing like this has ever happened before."

"Does Bobby have any symptoms?"

"Not that I'm aware of." Averting her eyes, the girl shook her head. "I mean, he looks the same and all."

Melissa noted her responses in her chart. No need to upset Sam until she knew for sure what was going on.

"Sam, I'm going to do a couple of tests on you. One is urinalysis, where I'll check your urine for infection, blood, and other things that would indicate problems. The second is a vaginal survey. This is where I'll make three microscope slides. I'll do a gram stain with one to check for bacteria. Do a saline prep with another slide to check for *Trichomonas pallidium*, which is a sexually transmitted disease, and I'll do a KOH slide to check for vaginal candidiasis, better known as a yeast infection."

Sam's lower lip trembled. "Will the tests hurt?"

"On the urinalysis, I'll need you to pee in a cup. For the vaginal survey, you'll have to have a pelvic exam similar to what it felt like when I did your Pap test," Melissa explained. She always used a liquid-based prep rather than the traditional Pap smear due to its increased accuracy and flexibility of testing for the human papillomavirus. "It'll be uncomfortable, but shouldn't be overly painful."

Twenty minutes later Melissa's suspicions were confirmed.

"Sam, the test showed that you have a *Trichomonas* infection." Melissa met the girl's wide eyes. "Like I mentioned earlier, this is a sexually transmitted disease."

"Oh, my God," Sam cried, covering her face with her hands. "I have an STD?"

"Yes, but fortunately it's treatable. *Trichomonas* is a parasite and will take a special type of anti-infective, but it will completely clear up." Melissa took a deep breath. "Sam, because you tested positive for this, you're at high risk of having other sexually transmitted diseases. I recommend you have blood tests for other STDs like genital herpes, hepatitis B, and HIV."

The crying girl shook her head in denial. "No, I can't have any of those because I've not been with anyone but Bobby. I was his first, too. I must have gotten this from a toilet seat or something."

"Sam, that isn't possible."

"But he doesn't have any symptoms."

"Men often don't show signs of sexually transmitted diseases." Which was unfortunate, but true.

"How could I have gotten this?"

Here came the whammie. "That's something you need to discuss with Bobby, but the logical answer would be that he's had sex with another person and infected you."

"No," came the sharp denial. "He loves me and wouldn't do that."

Melissa didn't say anything. Way too often she was the bearer of such bad tidings. Most women suspected something, but occasionally, and particularly with young girls, the news that their significant other had been unfaithful came as a total shock.

Was that why she'd leapt to conclusions so quickly in regard to James and Dr Weaver? Because she didn't want to be thought of as naïve? Not once prior to him telling her he was moving out had she questioned the nights he'd spent away from home. In her heart, she knew James hadn't cheated, wouldn't cheat on a woman he was involved with.

As long as he lived with her she stood a chance of changing his mind about her and their baby.

Thirty minutes and several blood tests later, Melissa walked into her office and dropped Sam's chart onto her desk.

Debbie quickly followed.

"I missed my appointment with Peggy."

Debbie gave an I've-got-your-back grin. "I told her you were hung up with a patient. She said not to worry about it and come when you could. She'll work you in."

Melissa glanced at her watch. If she hurried, she'd still have time to get the works and make it home by six. Without finishing her charting, she hurried out the door.

"Thanks, Debbie," she called over her shoulder to her friend. "Wish me luck."

"Wow. Dr James is gonna be one happy man when he gets a load of you," Peggy praised her handiwork.

Melissa had to admit that it had been months since

she'd looked so good. Not that the makeup completely hid the circles beneath her eyes, but almost.

Until she'd glanced in the mirror and seen the difference in how she looked compared to when she'd entered the salon, she hadn't realized how much she'd let herself go. Looks didn't matter that much when you were dealing with people's lives.

"I've got a dress in my shop that would look divine on you," Rhonda Peterson informed her from where another stylist was putting the finishing touches to her short curls. Rhonda ran a thrift store off Sawtooth's town square. "I picked it up on a shopping trip to Nashville. Still has the original tags and everything."

Which meant it had come from an upscale yard sale or another thrift shop. Rhonda was the queen of finding good deals.

"Oh, are you talking about that creamy number you got last week?" Gloria Stevens perked up from where she was reading a magazine, dozens of perm rollers tightly pinned to her head beneath a plastic cover.

"That's the one." Rhonda beamed.

"That dress is absolutely gorgeous." Gloria's gaze traveled over Melissa's trim figure. "And I bet it would fit perfectly."

The light in the women's eyes encouraged Melissa to at least take a look. She did want something different to wear tonight. Something breathtaking yet classy. Maybe Rhonda's dress was just the thing.

She glanced at her watch. Almost five. If she hurried, she'd have time to try on the dress and dazzle James when she walked in the door by six.

She paid Peggy for her hard work, then waited for Rhonda. Fifteen minutes later she stood in Rhonda's shop, slipping on what truly was a stunning silk dress. She half expected to look washed out, but with Peggy's expertly applied makeup, the neutral color of the dress made her eyes appear large, sultry. The peachy tones of her lipstick made her lips look pouty. The dress was the perfect final touch.

"Come on out here. Let me see what it looks like," Rhonda called from the other side of the dressing-room door.

Melissa stepped out.

Rhonda's eyes widened and a smug grin stretched across her face. "I knew that dress was made for you, but those shoes have got to go."

Melissa glanced down at her standard white walking shoes. "You have something that would work?"

"Oh, yeah, girl. I do. Come over here and let's try some on." Rhonda led her to a used shoe section that would rival any upscale department store. Most looked to be brand new or worn only once.

Melissa tried on three pairs of strappy high-heeled sandals before she found a pair she thought she could comfortably walk in and not break her neck. She told Rhonda as much.

"Honey, looking like you do, you aren't going to have to worry about doing much walking. Dr James will have you on your back in no time flat."

Guilt seized her. Rhonda, along with the women at the salon, must think she and James were planning a special night in. No wonder, since she'd gone to so much trouble with her appearance when they'd never known her to do so.

Even Debbie didn't know of James's request that morning, just that Melissa had decided to fight for her man.

"You think he's going to propose tonight?" Rhonda sounded wistful, as if she couldn't think of anything more romantic than James proposing.

That's when the truth struck Melissa. If James had proposed under the right circumstances, she couldn't think of anything more romantic either.

Under duress because she was pregnant lacked romance altogether. Particularly following his announcement that he was moving out.

She wanted the dream. James, babies, a happy home, and a happily-ever-after of her own.

Melissa shook her head. "Don't go starting rumors. We're just having a night in. It's been a while."

Rhonda nodded, but didn't look convinced. "With the way you work I don't know how y'all see each other at all. I'm glad you're taking some time for you and that scrumptious doctor friend of yours. You do so much for others. It's about time you did something for yourself."

Melissa smiled at Rhonda, thinking that she'd made some good friends in Sawtooth over the past few years.

Friends. Something she hadn't had during her childhood mainly because of the moves from one foster-family to another. After a while she'd just quit trying to make friends, but now she had them. When had that happened and why hadn't she realized? Because she'd been too busy to stop and smell the roses. Just like with James.

But wasn't it easier to focus on work than on the

problems with their relationship? With the fact that what she wanted was in direct opposition to what he wanted?

She touched her belly. She wanted their baby.

Remembering that Rhonda could be watching, Melissa blushed, paid for the dress and shoes, and waved goodbye. She'd just put her soiled clothes and walking shoes in the passenger seat of her car when her cell phone rang.

She looked at the number. Her office.

"Hello?"

"Are you still in town?" Debbie asked, sounding flustered.

"Yes. I'm outside Rhonda Peterson's shop. Why?"

"Jamie Moss is here. I was locking up the office when she arrived. Her youngest daughter had a bicycle crash and is bleeding everywhere. At least two of the cuts are going to need stitches. I've got pressure on the one on her knee but haven't been able to get the bleeding to stop." Debbie's sentences gushed out. "Jamie's a wreck. Her car wouldn't start and she had to run to a neighbor's to get a ride to the office, but he couldn't stay to drive her back home. What do you want me to do?"

Melissa closed her eyes. She could hear five-year-old Amanda screaming in the background, could hear Jamie's efforts to soothe the little girl. Could feel Debbie's frustration at having to call her tonight, knowing she planned to woo James.

Some things couldn't be helped and she couldn't send Amanda to an emergency room by ambulance when she knew the girl and her mother wouldn't have a way to get home. Not if she could take care of the problem in her clinic.

"I'll be there in two minutes."

It took three, thanks to getting caught at one of Sawtooth's four traffic lights.

Debbie had the girl in the procedure room and was applying pressure to a wound on her knee. Amanda screamed that she wanted her daddy and Jamie attempted to hug the girl, only to be pushed away.

Jamie burst into tears and Melissa went to her and placed her arms around the beaten-down woman.

"It's going to be OK. We'll get her sewn up and everything will be fine. She's just scared."

"I feel like such a failure. If I'd been watching her closer, she wouldn't have had the crash."

"Kids have bicycle crashes. It wasn't your fault."

"I want my daddy," the little girl wailed even louder, not liking being ignored by her mother and Melissa.

Jamie glanced toward her screaming daughter, then at Melissa. Horror filled her moist eyes. "I've gotten blood all over your pretty dress."

Despite the sinking feeling in her gut, Melissa held her expression in place. She hadn't given her dress a thought when she'd hugged Jamie and she wouldn't add to the woman's guilt.

"It's OK. It'll wash."

But not in time for her dinner with James.

She quickly assessed Amanda's injuries and calculated how long it would take. No way would she have Amanda sewn up and out of the office in time to make it home by six. Probably not by seven.

She glanced at her watch. Only minutes till six.

"I'm going to change into scrubs and decent shoes."

"Jamie, I need you to keep pressure on Amanda's knee while Debbie sets up a suture tray. Debbie, I'll need number four ethilon and, let's go ahead and give Amanda five milligrams of Valium to calm her down a bit."

Valium reminded her that she hadn't called to check on Wilma that afternoon, as she'd promised. She made a mental note to do so from her cell phone while driving home.

Melissa slipped into her bathroom and changed from the stained dress into a pair of blue scrubs. She caught sight of her reflection in the mirror. Gone was the excitement that had shone in her eyes at Peggy Williams's salon.

She loved her job, loved her patients, but she'd wanted to go home, to see desire flare in James's eyes when he looked at her, for him to see her as she would have looked and to want her with a passion that couldn't be subdued.

He'd be upset. She didn't blame him. Why would a good man like James keep putting up with a woman who was never there for him? And the reality of it was that she wasn't. Not that she'd realized it or meant it to happen, but James deserved better. And smart women like Dr Kristen Weaver were waiting to give it, and more, to him.

Knowing she didn't have time to dwell on the emotions swirling in her stomach, not when a little girl was bleeding, Melissa left the bathroom and picked up her phone.

Time to let James know she'd be late.

James surveyed the scene he'd set and liked what he saw. Last night, he'd gone about things all wrong. He'd realized that today.

Actually, Kristen had helped him to see the truth of the matter. She'd gawked when he'd said that he'd gone from telling Melissa he was moving out to saying they were going to get married. She'd pointed out that no woman would accept a shotgun marriage proposal that came on the heels of being dumped.

It struck him that he really hadn't proposed. He'd announced they were getting married. Melissa was way too independent for that to fly. Plus, she deserved the romance of him getting on his knees and asking her to share his life.

He hadn't planned to marry, but under the right circumstances marriage to Melissa could be good. Sure, the thought of becoming a parent scared the hell out of him, but he'd deal with it. He had no choice.

He inspected the deck once again, mentally checking off each detail. Melissa's favorite CD played low in the background. A dozen citronella candles burned in their various posts on the deck, but he'd placed a chunky beeswax candle in the center of the picnic table so the scent wouldn't interfere with their dinner.

He'd covered the table with a white cloth and set it with skills his mother had taught him at a young age. He'd picked up chicken breasts and thrown them on the grill about twenty minutes ago, letting them cook slowly. Vegetables steamed in the kitchen and were almost ready to be served. He'd even gotten a bottle of non-alcoholic cider champagne and had it chilling on the table.

It looked like a seduction scene. Not that that's what he was going for. He wanted to romance Melissa, not seduce her.

He patted his pocket, feeling the outline of the square jeweler's box. Tonight was all about romance. Now the one being romanced just had to do her part and come home.

On cue, the phone rang.

James glanced at his watch. Five minutes till six.

Denial punched him in the stomach, causing acid to bubble up his throat. No, she wouldn't, he thought, entering the house and seeing her name on the caller ID.

He couldn't bring himself to pick up the phone, as if not answering would somehow prevent her from canceling on their plans. She'd looked sincere that morning when she'd agreed to be home by six.

The answering machine came on. Melissa's voice filled the room.

"James, I'm not going to make it home until later tonight. An emergency's come up with a patient. I'm sorry. I'll be home as soon as I can."

Damn. She'd done it to him again.

How many times did it have to happen for him to know that he wasn't important to her?

Not that he believed she didn't care, but she didn't care enough. Not to where she could ever put his needs first.

Was this what their child would face time and again? Mommy not showing up for ball games and ballet recitals because a patient needed her?

Resolute, James walked back onto the deck and began blowing out candles. The box in his pocket burned through his slacks, scorching his skin, mocking him.

No more. He couldn't take this and Melissa was so caught up in her career that she didn't see what was happening. He dug into his pocket, fished out the box, and dropped it onto her place setting. Let her see what she'd lost when she came home to an empty house.

He was through playing second fiddle.

With that, he grabbed a few garbage sacks from the kitchen, walked into their bedroom, and began emptying his clothes drawers.

Perhaps it was too late for them to salvage their relationship other than to share custody of their baby. But maybe he could jolt her into waking up to reality before she tossed their child's needs aside, the way she continuously did his.

CHAPTER FOUR

"So, HOW did last night go?" Debbie asked with a sly grin when she walked into Melissa's office the next morning. Without waiting for an answer, she dropped the charts she carried onto the corner of Melissa's desk. "You sure don't look like you got any sleep."

Melissa opened her mouth but nothing came out.

Eyes narrowing, Debbie looked at her more closely. "Actually, you look like you cried all night."

There would be a reason for that.

When she didn't answer, Debbie placed her hand on Melissa's shoulder.

Biting her lower lip, Melissa fought tears she'd have sworn she'd exhausted during the long hours of the night. She couldn't cry. Not now. She was at the office.

"Oh, honey. I'm so sorry." Debbie squeezed her shoulder. "What did he say?"

Melissa stifled her pain. What was she doing? Self-pity wouldn't accomplish a thing. She'd learned that early on in the foster-care system. She sucked in a deep breath and pasted on what she hoped was a plausible smile.

"He was gone when I got home. No big deal."

"No big deal?" Her friend looked confused. "Hello? Are we in denial or what? We're talking about the man you love that you were going to fight to keep."

"I was going to fight for him, but apparently he knows what he wants, and it's not me." She kept a tight leash on the pain ricocheting through her. "I'd never force James into anything he doesn't want."

Debbie stared a long time, then shook her head. "I shouldn't have called last night. I should have taken Amanda to the ER myself."

"That's not your job."

"No, and it's not your job to always be available either." Debbie let out a long sigh. "I'm sorry for the role I played in this."

Melissa shook her head. Debbie hadn't known the significance of last night. "None of this is your fault and if you hadn't called me on Amanda, I'd have been upset. You did the right thing."

Debbie didn't look sure. "Did I?"

"Yes," Melissa answered, knowing in her heart that she told the truth. Amanda had needed her and Jamie had already had a rough day at the surgeon's office. "Dr Arnold will be doing a biopsy on Jamie's breast this afternoon. Poor thing."

Debbie stared at her strangely. "Are you OK?"

Her heart cried that she wasn't. Admitting that wouldn't accomplish anything except to earn Debbie's pity. She'd had her lifetime's fill of pity. She'd focus on work and she would be fine. It's what she'd always done.

"James leaving hurts, but life goes on." Knowing Debbie was watching her, Melissa picked up the charts and quickly dealt with reviewing the lab results. No more self-pity. No more tears. Not at the office, at any rate. Time enough for wallowing when she crawled into her big, empty bed tonight.

And every night to follow.

"What do we have on schedule for this morning?" she asked, eager to bury herself in distractions and escape Debbie's perplexed gaze.

The nurse shook her head, disappointment shining in her brown eyes. "You're double booked where we rescheduled yesterday afternoon's appointments. Room one is Riley Stokes with heartburn and indigestion. Room two is Mamie Thomas with bilateral foot numbness. Room three is Delilah Evans with upper respiratory symptoms."

"Guess I'd better get started, then." Grateful for the busy morning, Melissa grabbed her stethoscope, blamed her nausea on pregnancy, and headed to check on Riley Stokes.

Ten minutes later, she wrote out his prescription. "You have gastroesophageal reflux disease and esophagitis. That's where the acid in your stomach washes up into your esophagus. The esophagus isn't designed to handle the acid and it causes erosion of the tissue, which is why you hurt. The medicine I'm giving you is a proton pump inhibitor and it will decrease the amount of acid your stomach makes. It'll help the erosions to heal. Remember, though, you need to cut back on the spicy foods and don't lie down for at least an hour after you eat. Debbie will bring you a handout with other tips."

Mamie Thomas's foot numbness wasn't as simple to

treat. Mrs Thomas suffered from non-insulin-dependent diabetes, also known as type 2 diabetes, and had for at least thirty years. Unfortunately, she didn't adhere to a low-carbohydrate, high-protein diet and only took her medications sporadically.

Upon examination, Melissa found macerated skin between Mrs Thomas's toes and large callus formations. Using an instrument that looked like a hairbrush bristle, she checked Mrs Thomas's sensation. Not good. The diabetic couldn't even tell that the tine had touched her foot.

"Mrs Thomas, you have peripheral neuropathy that is caused by your diabetes. When your blood sugar runs high, it causes damage to the nerve endings. Over time, enough damage can occur to cause numbness."

"Can you fix it?" the elderly lady asked.

"No, I can't. However, if you'll take your medicines, it will help keep it from getting worse. There are also medicines that help to ease the accompanying burning sensation." She patted Mrs Thomas's hand. "I'm going to arrange for you to see a podiatrist, that's a doctor who specializes in feet. There's one in Dekalb, so your daughter won't have to drive you to Nashville."

The rest of Melissa's morning flew by, as did the afternoon. Not wanting to go home, she drove to Dekalb to check on Wilma. The mostly recovered widow had been released that morning to prepare for her husband's funeral the following day.

For the first time in weeks Melissa had nothing to keep her from going home.

She didn't want to go home. Didn't want to face the reality that James wouldn't be coming back.

Since she was already in Dekalb, she grabbed a yogurt and a bottle of water from a deli and then went to pick up household supplies.

She wound up in the baby section.

Browsing through the aisle, she touched this and read that. A soft floppy-eared rabbit with big oval eyes caught her attention and she picked it up, hugged it, and her eyes welled up.

The rabbit rode back to Sawtooth. Shopping bags and stuffed animal in hand, she entered the quiet house, wishing she'd left lights on that morning.

Lesson learned. Coming home to a dark, empty house was worse than coming home to an empty house.

Oh, who was she kidding? It was all bad.

Setting the rabbit on the counter, she put her other items away.

"Looks like it's just you and me tonight," she told the rabbit as she poured herself a glass of water. Not wanting to face the bed she'd shared with James, she hugged the stuffed animal, flipped on the outdoor light, and went through the French doors to sit on the deck.

And stopped short.

A white tablecloth covered the picnic table. Dew had settled onto the surface and a couple of bright leaves contrasted starkly against the tablecloth. A wheat-colored beeswax candle sat between two place settings. But it was the rectangular box on one of the plates that held her attention. A velvet-covered jeweler's box.

Her insides shaking, she picked it up. The soft fuzzy

covering felt damp in her hands. Her knees wobbled and she dropped into the closest chair.

Taking deep breaths and clinging to the stuffed rabbit, she opened the box and, despite knowing what it had to contain, she gave a strangled cry at what she saw.

A diamond ring.

An engagement ring.

James had bought her a ring.

She glanced around the candle-lined deck. She hadn't been the only one who had prepared for a special evening last night. James had bought her a ring and had planned to ask her to marry him. For real.

Then he'd left.

Left and taken his clothes.

Left to make the point that she'd put him off when he'd told her he needed her to be home.

Left the ring he was no longer willing to slip on her finger.

James closed the door to the doctors' lounge and was grateful to find the room empty. His insides ached too much to exchange pleasantries.

A newborn with respiratory syncytial virus had come into the emergency room. The infant had been sent over to the children's hospital, but the ill baby had reminded him of past failures. Failures that included the woman who would give birth to his flesh and blood.

Melissa's pregnancy had brought forth enough fresh waves of memories of Cailee, of him walking to her crib, thinking she was sleeping, and discovering something so horrible that it had forever changed the course of his life. Left him prostrate and knowing he never wanted to feel that helpless again. Cailee's death and his role in it had decided his future. He'd gone into medicine because never again would death snatch away someone so easily on his watch.

And although he'd looked death in the face many times, he hadn't gotten past losing Cailee and he suspected he never would. He avoided babies for just that reason.

Only time was running out for avoidance. Like it or not, he was Melissa's baby's father and he would do right by her.

He leaned against the cold concrete wall, rolling his forehead back and forth.

Three weeks and she hadn't called. She hadn't even acknowledged the ring or the fact that he'd left. Was she waiting for him to make the next move? To come home and beg her to take him back on any terms she'd have him?

The worst part was that he longed to do just that.

Maybe he would, except that meant facing issues he didn't want to face even beyond Cailee. Melissa was pregnant with his baby and was willing to let him walk away. Not only that, she'd given her blessing for him to start a relationship with another woman.

He clenched his fists and without any real force punched the solid wall.

She may as well have taken out a billboard that said he didn't matter.

Knowing he was a fool, he pulled his cell phone from his scrubs pocket and hit an auto-dial number.

"I thought I told you not to call me," a pert female voice said without bothering to say hello. He'd called so many times during the past weeks that Melissa's nurse recognized his cellular number and probably knew it from memory.

"Then tell me she's OK."

A soft sigh, then Debbie said in a resigned voice, "I told you I'd call if there were problems."

She had, along with telling him to quit calling her and to call Melissa directly. He couldn't do either.

"She's OK?"

"OK?" Debbie sighed. "Look, she's my boss and my best friend—it's wrong on so many levels for me to be talking to you."

"I just want to know that she's OK."

"She's pregnant and you dumped her. What else do you want to know?"

Was that how Melissa saw things? What she'd told Debbie had happened?

"I didn't dump her."

"Then where are you? Because you sure haven't been here for her the past couple of weeks, have you?"

Was he wrong? Or being selfish to want Melissa to care more for him? To place value on their relationship? No. He wasn't. But knowing he needed to stay away and being able to not check on her were two different things.

"She's eating?"

"Not much."

"Make her."

"You should know better than to tell me that."

Right. No one could make Melissa do anything unless it was what she wanted. "If she needs anything, you'll call?"

"She needs you to come home."

If only she really did. "I can't do that."

"No, I guess you're too busy."

Venom dripped from Debbie's words, giving James pause. Each time he called, Debbie's tone was full of sarcasm. Leaving had made him the bad guy. He could deal with that because leaving had been the right thing to do, even if he questioned that rightness a thousand times a day.

"Give me your word you'll call if anything happens."

"I told you I would. That hasn't changed." Debbie paused, then added, "Personally, I think you're both crazy."

James closed his cell phone and dropped it back into his pocket. He wouldn't argue about his foolishness. What kind of man resorted to calling a woman's best friend just to make sure she was OK?

Not one he liked falling into the same category with, that was for sure.

Ignoring the woman studying him, James scribbled a note on the document he was scanning.

"It's been a month, James. Are you or are you not going to tell me what happened?" Kristen leaned across the counter. When he continued to ignore her, she tapped on the paper. "James, I asked you a question."

"I already told you, I don't want to talk about it." Calling Debbie for information daily was bad enough.

"You haven't said anything about what happened, and I know it couldn't have been good. For that matter, you haven't said much of anything, period. You just walk around all roboticlike, holding everything in, and I've had enough of it." When he continued to ignore her, she jerked the pen out of his hand and tossed it onto the counter with a resounding whack. "I want my friend back."

James watched the pen flip, then roll across the counter and drop to the floor. He ran his fingers through his hair, looked around the laboratory he and Kristen used for their research. Three high-tech computers topped one counter. Another counter ran the entire length of the room and curved halfway around the adjacent wall. Two double sinks broke the monotony. Cabinets hung above the counters, more rested below them. Models of hearts were crammed into a corner. Numerous anatomy posters lined what free wall space there was. Nothing fancy, but they didn't need fancy.

"Look, I've had a rough few weeks and prefer not to have this conversation." Hoping she'd take a hint, he picked up the pen and made more notes.

"It's a proven fact that talking helps." She tapped her short, unpolished fingernail against the countertop and gave her bossiest look. "So talk."

"Since when did you get a PhD in psychology?"

"My specialty is hearts. Do you think I can't see that yours is breaking? I've given you space. At first I thought that's what you needed, but you're not getting any better." Her green eyes searched his, saw that she had his attention. "Talk to me, James. Let me help."

"There's nothing to say."

"I take it Melissa refused your proposal?"

Why had he told Kristen about his plans that night? Because he'd been so damned sure Melissa would accept and that he'd become a married man.

James snorted. "Technically, she didn't refuse."

"Then you're engaged?" She looked skeptical. "Because with the way you've acted I would have sworn things hadn't gone well."

Kristen was on a mission. He knew her too well to think she'd let up now that she'd given voice to the questions in her eyes. They'd stayed behind, analyzing data collected from six major trauma hospitals and putting finishing touches on their work. She'd been watching him, biding her time.

"I left before she came home," he admitted.

"You left?" Kristen's dark brow rose. "You bought a diamond the size of Texas and left without giving it to her?"

"She didn't come home. She called and canceled."

"Canceled?"

He stooped, picked up his pen before giving a nonchalant shrug. "She said something came up with a patient."

Kristen gave him a speculative look. "Did you ever stop to think that perhaps it really did?"

James shoved away from the work space and paced across the lab, flicking a paper clip along the length of the countertop with his pen. "I'm sure it did."

Kristen followed him. "Then what's the problem?"

"That's just it." He turned, facing her. "There's always a patient, always someone who needs her more. She's a great doctor and gives one hundred percent of who she is to her patients. There's nothing left for me."

"Have you told her how you feel?" Kristen touched his shoulder. "That you need her?"

James cringed. He didn't want Kristen's sympathy.

He didn't want to be having this conversation. "When was I supposed to do that? She's always at work."

"Maybe you should book an appointment."

He rolled his eyes. "Very funny."

"I'm serious," she said, giving him a soft smile. "I've never known you to give up so easily."

"Give up?" he scoffed. "I didn't give up a damned thing. I walked away."

"Give up. Walk away. Whatever you want to call it."

"You don't understand." He sounded like a whiny kid.

"You're right. I don't. How could a man who will work thirty minutes trying to bring life back to a flat-lining heart walk away from his own heart's desire?" She touched his face, placing her finger over his mouth when he started to deny what she'd said. "Don't even say it because we both know she's who you want. Once upon a time I hoped, but I know hearts." She let her finger drag across his chin, then fall to her side. "And yours belongs to Melissa."

She was one of his best friends and a trusted colleague, but he'd never felt anything more for her.

"I'm sorry." He felt like a heel.

"Don't be." Sadness shone in her eyes, but she smiled. "It's not your fault."

Why couldn't he have fallen for Kristen? They had so much in common. In that moment he wondered if he could make himself forget Melissa by focusing on Kristen. What would it feel like to kiss her?

Like he was cheating. Because, no matter what his mind said, his heart did belong to Melissa. He'd not wanted anyone else since first setting eyes on her at a medical meeting they'd both attended on asthma.

He'd made some corny comment about her taking his breath away and she'd offered to do mouth-to-mouth. They'd shared a smile, a laugh, a look full of awareness, and the rest, as they said, was history.

Only their history had taken a drastic turn in the wrong direction.

God, he missed her. Missed the way her eyes opened slowly in the mornings, the way she stretched the sleep from her body, missed the way she said his name when they made love.

"James."

God, now he was hearing things. But if he was, Kristen imagined it, too, because her gaze moved to behind him where he instinctively knew Melissa stood. No one else made his heart hammer like a wildebeest stampede across the Serengeti.

He turned.

Glancing back and forth between him and Kristen, Melissa stood just inside the doorway. Hurt and accusation blanched her face.

Thank God, she'd finally come.

Kristen stepped back. "I'm going to call it a night." She got her purse from a cabinet and shot him a quick glance. "Remember what I said, James. I'll talk to you tomorrow."

He nodded, his gaze remaining on Melissa. How could someone look so good and so bad all at the same time?

"Nice to see you, again," Kristen acknowledged as she walked past the thin woman. "Congrats on your pregnancy."

Melissa's gaze grew more accusing. Had she not wanted him to tell anyone she was pregnant? Did she think no one would notice the soft swell beneath her blue blouse? Or, despite her weight loss, how her breasts were fuller?

When Kristen was gone, Melissa closed the door. The door that usually would have been closed, but he'd been distracted.

Once they were alone in the room, she seemed unsure what to say. Awkward seconds passed.

"I have an ultrasound scheduled for tomorrow morning here at Vanderbilt. For the baby," she clarified. "Dr McGowan wants to confirm my due date as my last period was so scanty. Based on that and his palpation of my uterus, he thinks I'm five months pregnant rather than four."

Five months? James felt the blood drain from his face. He studied her belly more closely, wondering if it was possible. He'd have even less time to cope with becoming a father. He didn't speak, just waited for her to tell him why she'd come.

She hesitated, closed her eyes, and took a deep breath. "I thought you might like to be there. For the ultrasound, I mean."

"OK." He wasn't sure how he was going to deal with a baby, but if Melissa wanted him there, he'd go.

She appeared surprised at his quick answer. He bit his tongue and waited.

"I'm really sorry about that night." Standing in front of the door, clenching and unclenching her fingers, she looked frail, unsure of herself. "I wanted to be home."

"It's OK."

"No, it's not." She blew out a pent-up breath. "If it had been OK, you'd have been there when I got home."

"True," he admitted, wondering why he'd said it was OK to begin with. Nothing about falling at the end of Melissa's priority list was OK.

CHAPTER FIVE

JAMES fought telling Melissa just how un-OK her not coming home had been. At this point, what did it matter? She'd made her bed, now was the time to lie in it. Wasn't that his intention?

"You packed your clothes," she said, watching him closely.

"Yes." If tossing his things into garbage bags that still lined a friend's spare bedroom wall counted as packing.

"You're not coming back, are you?" Her voice wobbled, but her gaze remained steady, boring into him with their chocolate depths.

It would be so easy to give in, to beg her to let him come home. They could kiss and make up and pretend everything was fine. It's what he wanted to do. Particularly the kissing and making up part.

Going home wouldn't solve anything. It would just expose his heart to the next round of her careless arrows.

But, looking at her, seeing the hesitation in her eyes, he yearned to take her in his arms and kiss away the pain.

"No," he answered, knowing the best gift he could give Melissa was to open her eyes. The best gift he could give a son or daughter he was afraid of was to make sure Melissa put their child first in her life. "I'm not coming back."

Her gaze lowered to the floor and she reached out to grasp hold of a countertop as if she was dizzy.

He started to go to her, but she steadied and he held himself back.

Just seeing her ripped the scabs off his wounds, made his insides ache. No matter how important she was to him, he needed more than she was willing to give. She'd proved that time and again.

He had to stand his ground.

She dug in her pocket and pulled out a box. The jeweler's box he'd left on the deck.

"Then you should take this."

James watched her set the box on the counter. Her fingers shook and she slid them into her pants pockets. Her gaze lifted to his. The unhappiness he saw there undid everything but the need to comfort her.

He crossed the room to stand in front of her, stared down at her, and couldn't resist touching her cheek.

His body screamed that this was Melissa and why wasn't he pulling her to him? Showing her how much he wanted her? How happy he was to see her? He managed to restrain himself to brushing his fingertips over her smooth skin.

"Why are you here, Melissa?"

She trembled, giving testament to how much coming here had cost her emotionally. Her eyes closed, and she swayed slightly into his touch. "I told you."

"Tell me again."

Her lower lip disappeared into her mouth. "I want you with me when I have my ultrasound."

She wanted him with her. Not just that she was having it and he could tag along if he wanted. Progress.

"I'll be there." If it ripped his insides apart, and it damned well might, he would be there. "What else?"

She blinked. "What do you mean?"

"You didn't drive an hour to ask me to go to your ultrasound." Saying the words gave them credence. She could have called, but hadn't.

"I was in town for my appointment with Dr McGowan, but—" she met his gaze "—I wanted to see you."

His heart flopped in his chest like a fish out of water.

"Why?" Deep down he knew the answer, but wanted to hear her say the words out loud. Needed to hear her say them.

"I miss you."

Yes.

"We barely saw each other," he reminded her perversely. "Between the nights I stayed in Nashville and your work schedule, I'm surprised you noticed I was gone."

She leaned toward him, pressed her palms against his chest. "I noticed."

His pulse raced so rapidly he expected someone to wave black-and-white checkered flags at any moment. Having her touch him, even through his scrubs, made him feel like a winner. It also reminded him of what he'd lost, yet he wouldn't yield, not on something so important.

"I want you to come home."

His heart said yes. His lips said, "No."

She must have known his heart, because her eyes

widened in surprised hurt. "You never gave me reason to think you were unhappy. Not until the night before you left. Why won't you come home?"

"My home is in Nashville. It always has been." He pulled back, stepping away from her closeness before her sweet vanilla scent caused him to nuzzle closer. "My moving in with you was never meant to be permanent."

Thick lashes swept her cheeks. "It wasn't?"

"No." He'd meant to convince her to move to Nashville, become a part of his life. At the time he'd been spending so much time in Sawtooth that more and more of his things had ended up at Melissa's. When she'd asked him to move in, it had made sense to let his apartment go, rather than continue to drive back and forth.

Because she hadn't been willing to budge on where she belonged. In Sawtooth.

Her hands fell to her sides and she paced across the room. "I see."

Somehow James doubted she did, at least not the truth. That their relationship was too precious to allow it to be treated as an afterthought, there for her convenience and nothing more.

She spun, pinned him with an angry glare. "So I was right?"

Color stained her cheeks and her eyes glittered. She looked more like the woman he'd fallen for than she had in months. Alive, vibrant, aware that he existed as a man.

She was aware. He felt it in her radiating energy, saw it in the way she looked at him with hungry eyes that said she saw a desirable man, one she'd like to tackle right here, right now.

God, he wanted to kiss her, touch her. But if he did, he'd lift her onto the countertop, peel away her clothes, and make love to her. One touch and he wouldn't be able to stop.

He shoved his hands into his scrubs pockets. "About?"

"You and Dr Weaver." She sounded jealous. "You looked—what's the right word?—close when I arrived."

Possessiveness shone brightly in her dark eyes and, despite his body's protest at his denial of its yearnings, his spirits lifted.

"We are close." Which was true enough. Kristen was one of his best friends. Until moments before Melissa had arrived he hadn't known she'd wanted more, but that didn't change the friendship they shared. Neither did it mean he had to reveal to Melissa that there would never be anything more than friendship between Kristen and him. Melissa's brown eyes turned green went a long way to soothe his bruised ego.

"You've moved in with her?"

"No, I'm staying with one of the residents I had in class last year."

"A female?"

He bit back a smile. "No, the one I stayed with on the nights I worked late. Ted Jefferson. You've met him."

Melissa paced across the room, her whole body screaming with agitation and tension.

"Has she—" the pronoun came out high-pitched "—offered to let you stay with her?"

"What does that have to do with anything?"

"Which means she has." Her tone bounced between defeatist, determined, and accusatory.

He had to make a stand, to play hardball, otherwise he and Melissa would both end up losers. So, praying for strength, he reminded her of the basic facts. "When you opted not to come home the other night, you ended our personal relationship. Where I stay isn't your concern."

She sucked in a deep breath. Her face grew ghastly pale and guilt hit him. Why feel guilty? He'd spoken the truth. He was a free man and could sleep anywhere he liked. Do whatever he liked. Not that he would even if she weren't pregnant.

The baby. He swallowed the lump in his throat. Was that why he'd run so quickly? Kristen had accused him of giving up. Had he given up or run scared? No, Melissa had pushed him aside. The baby had had nothing to do with him leaving.

He'd been taking a stand, a difficult but necessary one.

"I'm not rushing into anything, but make no mistake—" he stared straight into her dismayed eyes "—I have no intention of remaining celibate. There will be other women in my life."

She stepped back, leaned against the counter. "I made a mistake, coming here."

"What did you expect? That you could say you were sorry and I'd come running back to be available whenever you had time to fit me into your schedule?"

The look on her face said that's exactly what she'd thought. No. Hell no.

"As the mother of my baby, you'll always be a part of my life, but you willingly gave up the right to any say in what I do."

She didn't comment, just clutched the countertop. He didn't want to hurt her, had never wanted her to hurt. So why was he trying to make her jealous?

Because jealousy meant she cared, and he wanted her to care. But her painful, devastated expression gutted him.

"Look, it can't be good for the baby for you to get upset." Actually, her reaction surprised him. If she cared so much, why hadn't she made an effort to be there for him? He'd told her how much he'd needed her to come home that night. "What is it you want of me, Melissa?"

"To come home," she immediately responded, almost echoing his former sentiments.

"Sawtooth has never been my home." That wasn't completely true. In the beginning, he had been happy wrapped in the warmth of her attention and the life they'd started carving out for themselves. What had changed?

"Because you wouldn't let it be. How many times did I ask you to give the office a chance? To get to know my patients so you'd understand how I feel about them?"

"That's just it, Melissa," he sighed. "I do understand. Which is why I'm back in Nashville. Your patients need you. But not only that." The thought had hit him with such clarity he felt a fool for not seeing it sooner. "You need them to need you."

"I need *you*."

"Then I feel badly for you." If he believed her, things would be different, but he didn't. Words came cheap and actions spoke loud.

"What about the baby?"

Which was the real clincher in all this. The wrench

he hadn't counted on when he'd made the decision to shake up their relationship.

"What about the baby?" he repeated, trying to remain logical and not let his heart lead him astray. He'd focus on the baby he'd never wanted and that he worried she'd never be there for because she'd be running to one patient after another. "We'll talk to a lawyer and come up with a compromise on custody. A plan we can both live with, hopefully both be happy with. Keeping things civil between us works to everyone's advantage."

He managed to sound calm, even though his insides twisted.

Her eyes widened with fear and outrage. "A lawyer?"

Did she expect him to pretend he didn't know she carried his baby? He may not have wanted to be a father, to carry that kind of responsibility, but no way in hell would he walk away from his child.

Of course, Melissa had no idea he checked on her daily so maybe she believed he had turned his back on her.

"It would be in our best interests for us to have custody legalized." His baby would have his name. No matter what, he'd insist upon that. "Surely you see that?"

She gawked at him. "Are you saying you're going to try to take my baby away from me?"

"Our baby," he reminded her, annoyed that she was trying to cut him out of even that. "And, no, that's not what I said. Joint custody, Melissa. I'd never keep our child from knowing his or her mother."

"But you think I might?" she scoffed. "That's why you want a lawyer?"

"No," he sighed. "I don't think you'd try to keep our

baby from me. You've been honest about your pregnancy, even after I gave you reason not to be." He studied her for a moment, taking in her glistening eyes. "It couldn't have been easy to tell me you're pregnant after I said I was moving out."

"No," she admitted, averting her gaze, attempting to hide the raw hurt. "It wasn't."

Had she thought he'd stay? That she could live her life just as it was and he'd be there whenever she decided to toss some attention his way? Their baby's way?

Why wouldn't she? It's what they'd been doing for months.

She'd been right about him not saying anything until that fateful night. Which made him wonder why he hadn't. Had he been willing to accept the status quo just to keep her in his life? Up till that night when he'd discovered another person—their baby—would face the repercussions of his cowardice at facing a lonely, broken heart.

"You had a right to know about our baby." She bit her lower lip. "I couldn't not tell you."

She shivered and he wondered what had run through her mind when she'd told him about their baby.

"Look, it's late and I haven't eaten. Do you want to grab a bite to eat?" He glanced around the lab, wondering what the hell he was doing and, better yet, *why*.

"I'm not sure that's a good idea." Apparently she questioned the wisdom of their dining together, too. Still, he wanted to get out of the lab, to get her off her feet and some food in her belly.

"We need to talk, to try to figure out what it is we want regarding the baby." They really did have a lot to discuss. Things they should decide before involving a third party.

"OK," she agreed, although he could tell it was with reluctance.

"Good. You need to eat."

She gave him a disgusted look. "Not you, too."

"Debbie giving you a hard time?" he asked, grinning, trying to lighten the mood. Although confused about the emotions running though him, he couldn't stand to see her so stressed. Besides, spending the evening with her would only show her that much more what she'd lost.

Looking puzzled at his olive branch, she nodded. "Hopefully the nausea will pass soon, but until then I'm condemned to listen to her complain about my weight."

"You're too thin," he said, causing her to frown. There he went, upping the tension again. Not that he'd meant to but, hell, she was too thin.

Her spine went ramrod straight. "Thanks."

"I just meant that you've lost weight when you should be gaining it."

Her chin lifted. "Lots of women lose weight during the first stages of pregnancy."

"Four, maybe five months is past the first stages, don't you think?" He raked his gaze over her slender frame. Despite the bulge at her midsection, her clothes hung loosely and her bones were too prominent. "How much have you lost? Ten pounds? Fifteen?"

"Doesn't matter. I'll put it back on."

"What did Dr McGowan say when you saw him?"

"That I need to eat more, but I'm healthy. He doesn't expect any complications."

Her gaze wouldn't meet his and she hesitated just long enough that he knew Dr McGowan hadn't glossed over her weight as much as she let on.

"Does he know I'm the father?"

"He asked how you were, so I assume he knows. I listed you as my emergency contact." Her face wrinkled in thought. "I did it without thinking, then second-guessed whether or not I should have since we're not together, but I'd written in ink."

How had things become so awkward between them?

Him moving out of the house and an unplanned pregnancy. That's how.

"It's fine," he assured her, shutting down the computer and locking up his and Kristen's notes inside a cabinet. "I want to know if there's any problems."

But Melissa looked uncomfortable and, whether or not it fit with his desire for her to see what she'd lost, he swore that before the night was over he'd ease the worry lines furrowing her forehead.

How could he not? Her health and well-being was the health and well-being of their baby.

Going to dinner with James had been a mistake. A huge mistake.

The entire evening had been a huge mistake.

Why had she gone to where she knew she'd find him? After her appointment with Dr McGowan, she should have driven home. For that matter, why had she opted to go to an obstetrician in Nashville rather than at much closer Dekalb?

Well, Dr McGowan did do her yearly gynecological

exam, so maybe James wouldn't assume it had anything to do with him.

It didn't have anything to do with him.

She sneaked a glance at him. He stared straight ahead, watching the late evening traffic. Thick lashes shielded his eyes and his jaw flexed with tension. His dark hair had grown out enough that it curled at the ends. She itched to touch the soft strands. Itched to touch him, period.

Her entire body had shaken when she'd put her hands on his chest in the lab.

Of course, she'd also shaken when she'd walked in to find James and Kristen practically in each other's arms. He'd been looking at the cardiologist with deep emotion.

The muscles in Melissa's chest clamped down and she struggled to breathe. James was an attractive man, a good man. Dr Weaver wouldn't hold the exclusive on wanting him. Whether or not he wanted children, whether or not he hid his heart behind walls, women would line up to catch his eye and count their lucky stars if he glanced their way.

She'd had his eye, his attention, and she'd let a desire for a baby blind her to what she and James had shared. Now, by the grace of God, she would have his baby, but no longer had any other claim over the most important man to ever enter her life.

He'd announced they were getting married and she'd said no. *Idiot.* But how could she have said yes when the only reason he'd asked had been because of the baby?

But, then, had she told him about the baby in the hope he'd not leave? Sure, ethics played a role, but had she secretly hoped James would polish his armor and come riding in on his trusty white steed?

But he hadn't swept her off her feet because she hadn't been around for him to do any sweeping. When all was said and done, she'd be left to face each day alone. And she couldn't blame anyone but herself.

"You OK?" Blue eyes stared at her, then quickly glanced at the road and back.

"I'm not sure my dinner agreed with me." What was she supposed to say? That she felt like she was dying on the inside? That she missed him and wanted him to come home? Wait, she had said that.

He'd said no.

A sob gurgled up her throat and she bit it back, turning to stare out the window at the Twenty-First Avenue traffic.

"You didn't eat enough for it to have upset your stomach."

She turned, noticed his white-knuckled grip on the leather-coated steering wheel and wondered at his tension.

"Why?" she asked, before giving thought to her words. "Why did you have to leave me?"

Was that desperation she heard in her voice? She hated it, felt reduced to the lonely little girl she'd once been, begging for someone to love her, *anyone*. She'd survived then, learned to rely on herself, to throw herself into other things and excel at them. School first, then work. That had been enough. Until James. Until she'd begun to crave what he wouldn't give her and had once again thrown herself into a working frenzy to distract herself from the emotional deficits in her life.

And now what? Was she going to snivel and beg for his love? Not during this lifetime. She lifted her chin.

"I shouldn't have said that. We've discussed why you left and that you don't want to come home. Now we have to figure out how we're going to handle being parents that live in separate households, a subject we managed to completely avoid discussing during dinner." They'd talked about Wilma Barnes, about his new students, about her appointment with Dr McGowan, about the raccoon who kept getting into the garbage, but not about any of the issues between them. "I'm sure we can come to an understanding."

He didn't say anything for a long time, just pulled into the Vanderbilt parking garage where she'd parked. He found a space near her car.

"How do you propose we do that?" He sounded distant, like he'd added another layer to that protective wall he hid behind.

She bit the inside of her lip, laid her hand over her protruding belly and sighed. "I'm not sure, but there has to be a way we can both be happy because, despite what you may think, I do want you to be happy, James."

Although, watching him stare at the dashboard, looking so unlike the man she'd once laughed with, held in her arms, and woken up next to, she wondered if *she'd* ever be happy again.

CHAPTER SIX

As PROMISED the night before, James met Melissa in the hospital waiting room and accompanied her to her sonogram appointment. A hundred times he'd considered backing out, had woken up in a cold sweat during the night with the reality of what he'd agreed to do.

He didn't want to see his baby, didn't want that image mixing with Cailee's.

But he had no choice. He'd given Melissa his word. So here he stood, bracing himself for what he'd soon see on the screen, while the ultrasound technician rolled the wand over Melissa's protruding belly. He stared haplessly at Melissa's stomach, hoping he didn't throw up—or, worse, pass out.

Because he couldn't recall ever feeling this clammy, this weak-kneed. Well, yes, he could recall another time he'd felt this bad, and worse. When Cailee died.

Gel shone slickly on Melissa's goosebumped skin. How could she be cold when he was sweating like a horse?

Straining her neck to see the screen, Melissa watched the monitor with awe on her face. Awe and protectiveness. It did his heart good to see her maternal instincts coming out. Because, during the long hours of his restless night, he'd decided the best thing he could do for their baby was to make sure Melissa took care of herself and to teach her not to let her career overwhelm every aspect of her life. That way she'd reach her potential of being a great mother, because he didn't think he'd be a good father. How could someone who was afraid to care about a baby be a good dad?

"Amazing," Melissa said, her voice hoarse with emotion.

He didn't want to look. He really didn't. Yet the light in her eyes, the look of pure love, suckered him in. What on the screen was so powerful as to completely entrance Melissa? Bracing himself, James looked, expecting familiar guilt to wash over him, expecting the image of Cailee's face to overwhelm him.

Instead, he saw a tiny little person moving with an energy that defied the confines of Melissa's belly. He watched in amazement as the baby carried on moving, oblivious to its spectators.

Unexpectedly, his fingers itched to touch the screen, to make contact with the baby. His baby. The child he and Melissa made together.

He didn't want a baby. Knew he didn't want one. Would argue till hell froze over that he never wanted kids.

Yet when he looked at the ultrasound monitor, saw the tiny person he'd helped make, he wanted it. Wanted with all his being for their baby to be healthy and happy and have a wonderful life. He knew deep in his gut that he'd move heaven and earth to make that happen.

His baby.

He held himself tense for fear of thoughts of Cailee. Thoughts that didn't come. Instead, his thoughts focused on the tiny heart beating, the most precious gift he'd ever received.

With that tiny beating heart also came great fear. How could he take a chance on being responsible for a baby? On risking the devastation his parents had endured? The devastation he'd endured? What if he messed up and Melissa had to endure that pain because of *him*?

He wanted to take her in his arms, tell her all the wild thoughts bombarding him, tell her about Cailee. He'd almost told her once. Not long after he'd moved in with her, they'd been lying in bed in the afterglow of making love.

"James, do you see us having babies and growing old together someday?" she'd asked, lazily trailing her fingers over his bare chest. But there hadn't been anything lazy in her gaze. There had been longing, longing for things he hadn't wanted and a new fear had seized him. A fear that he might lose her.

"I can't imagine ever not wanting to be with you, Melissa, but we don't need babies to be happy. Not as long as we have each other."

She'd raised herself up on her elbows, stared at him oddly. "You really don't want kids? A girl who looks like you, a boy who looks like me?"

He'd rubbed his hand over his stubble-strewn jaw. "I don't. If that's where you see us going, I have to warn you otherwise. I won't ever have kids."

Her eyes had widened. "You can't have kids?"

"I don't choose to."

"Why not? You'd make such a wonderful father, James."

And that's when he started to tell her about Cailee. He wouldn't make a good daddy. He wasn't even able to keep an eye on his three-month-old sister for two hours while his parents went out for the evening. Friends stopped by and Cailee was sleeping in her crib, so he thought nothing of the hour he spent shooting the breeze on the front porch. After all, if Cailee woke up, he'd hear her through the open doorway. Only she didn't wake up and when, his friends having gone, he finally checked on her, she wasn't breathing, and despite his frantic but unskilled efforts, nothing he did revived her. By the time the paramedics arrived, it was too late. The medical examiner ruled it as SIDS, sudden infant death syndrome, but James knew her death was his fault. If he'd been watching her, if he'd known what to do, he could have saved her, and he hadn't. It was his fault Cailee died. His fault that his parents couldn't heal from the loss and divorced less than six months later.

"I can't think of anything I'd less want to be than a daddy." He'd sat up, pulling Melissa to him so he could look into her eyes. "There will never be kids if you spend your life with me. If you can't live with that, we should end this now, before either of us gets hurt."

He'd waited with bated breath for her answer.

"But why? Why wouldn't you want babies?"

Again, he'd considered telling her about Cailee. But what if Melissa couldn't care for a man directly responsible for a baby's death? What if she left him because of his negligence? After all the official reports, he'd never spoken of Cailee to anyone. Just the thought of saying her name out loud had been enough to convince him not to start now.

"The world is a horrible place," he'd said instead. "There's war, crime, hatred, diseases, overpopulation—Shall I go on? I don't need children to validate my existence. The basic fact is that I don't want kids. If you do, if I'm not enough, we should call it quits now."

She'd stared at him for the longest time, then leaned forward and placed a gentle kiss on his lips. "I want you, James."

"I'm serious, Melissa." He'd needed to know she agreed, that she'd be with him without pressuring him for things he didn't want.

"So am I. I want to be with you, James. Always."

Always, she'd said, and he'd thought everything would be fine.

How wrong he'd been.

"Do you want to know the sex of your baby?" the technician asked, causing James to blink, realize that he'd gotten caught up in the past and forgotten where he was, what was happening.

His gaze met Melissa's. Had she been watching him while he'd reminisced about days gone by? Confusion shone in her eyes. No wonder. He felt damned confused himself, mostly by his own reactions. They'd agreed on no kids and yet… He swallowed the knot in his throat.

"No," Melissa answered, still studying him with bright eyes that saw too much.

"Yes," James said at the same time, surprising himself at the admission. Particularly as he hadn't

known until that moment that he wante
thing he possibly could about their ba

He glanced at the screen and wi
emotions prickling in his chest. Moistu

The baby moved, spread its legs, co
ing any question of gender.

"Couples disagree about this all
problem." The ultrasound tech clicked a mou
times, recording measurements. "If you want to kno
I'll walk down to the ER later and tell you, Dr Stanley."

"I already know," James confessed, watching the
baby seem to look directly at him. Impossible.

Oblivious to the turmoil rolling through James, the
tech grinned as he repositioned the device on Melissa's
belly. "I kinda figured you hadn't missed the perfect
view we got. This little one isn't bashful. The hard part
is keeping it a secret when Mom doesn't want to know."

Fighting being overwhelmed with emotion, James
told himself to grow up. "Mom knows."

"I don't." Melissa shook her head. "Promise you
won't tell me."

No way could she have missed that view. Not if she'd
been looking at the screen. Which meant she hadn't
been. *She'd still been watching him.* Was that why she
stared at him like he'd grown a second head? Because
she'd seen his bewilderment? Could she tell how scared
he was of a being that was mere inches long?

He didn't say anything, just went back to watching
the screen. Because looking at Melissa, letting her green
eyes probe his, made him feel like she could see everything, made him feel impotent and weak. Hell, babies

n impotent and weak, made everyone weak
their lives depended on you and if you screwed
y died.

ailee should be whacking him with memories, with
grets, but he couldn't pull the image forward,
wondered why he even attempted to. Instead, he became
mesmerized by his baby, who was sucking its thumb.

"So precious," Melissa whispered, her hand reaching
out, clasping James's.

He couldn't even acknowledge that she'd touched
him. Only that he'd helped create a miracle.

"Yes." The word came out as a growl. He hadn't meant
it to, but his entire insides had puffed up, including his
voice box. That was his baby. His. His and Melissa's.

The radiologist handed Melissa a paper towel to clean
the gel off her belly and her hand fell away from his, un-
acknowledged. Her mouth formed a tight line and he
could tell that his lack of response upset her. Couldn't she
tell how overwhelmed he felt? How he was bursting with
joy and pride and scared to death all at the same time?

On the night after her ultrasound Melissa got a call from
James. And each night following. They didn't talk long
or discuss any issues. He asked how she felt, if she was
eating, if she'd felt the baby move. Fine, yes, yes, came
her nightly replies. She wanted to say more, but the
right words never came out. Maybe the right words
didn't exist.

James wanted to know what was happening with her
pregnancy. He wanted her to be healthy. He may not
have wanted a baby, may not even realize the truth, but

he'd fallen in love with the precious soul within her. A love that he failed to shield behind the fortress around his heart, perhaps because he hadn't expected the emotion to hit him. A deep love that she'd never seen in his gaze before.

She rejoiced and ached all at once. She wanted him to love their baby, but hadn't been prepared for her jealousy. What was wrong with her? She'd never been a jealous kind of person, but these days she practically breathed green fire.

She'd been so lost in watching him, wondering what had caused the color to drain from his face and his hands to tremble, that she'd missed the perfect view. Which was just as well because she really didn't want to know the baby's gender. Although if it had been that easy to tell, she suspected their baby must be a boy.

A son. A little boy who looked like his daddy. How would her heart ever take that? He'd surely wrap her around his little finger and she'd never be able to deny him a thing.

Two weeks passed without her seeing James. Just the nightly phone calls.

The pressure of taking off work for her appointment with Dr McGowan and for the ultrasound put her behind schedule. She still didn't feel she'd caught up, and although her nausea had passed and she was beginning to eat well again, fatigue set in, making her schedule that much more difficult. Plus, she hadn't slept well since James moved out. All in all, stress was taking its toll on her body.

Perhaps tonight she'd get home in time for a long, warm bath. Maybe that would relax her enough for sleep.

But before she thought about baths and sleep, she needed to finish seeing her patients for the day. The morning clinic had been full of kids from the local elementary school ill with a stomach virus and this afternoon wasn't proving any slower.

She glanced at the chart in her hand. Amanda Moss. Way later than the recommended seven to ten days, but no doubt at the office to have her stitches removed.

Guilt hit Melissa. Why hadn't she thought to drive out to Jamie's trailer and remove the stitches?

"Hi, Amanda. How's that knee?" she asked, entering the room. Immediately, her eyes were drawn to the pale woman sitting in the chair next to the exam table.

Jamie looked terrible. Much worse than the harrowed reflection that stared back at Melissa each time she gazed in a mirror—and that was saying something.

Jamie's eyes were puffy and already her eyebrows had become scanty from her chemotherapy. The cheap wig covering her head wouldn't have fooled a blind man. Her face was swollen. But it was the lost expression in Jamie's eyes that broke Melissa's heart.

"It hurts." Amanda pouted, putting both hands over her knee and giving Melissa a suspicious glare.

Jamie's sad eyes went to her youngest daughter. "She doesn't want them taken out. I know I should have gotten her here sooner, but I…" Her voice trailed off. "I just didn't have the energy to do more than go for my chemotherapy and run the girls back and forth to school."

"I know you're doing the best you can," Melissa assured her, eyeing the tightly embedded sutures.

Deciding to care for Amanda first, as she was the actual patient, Melissa placed the chart on the countertop and washed her hands. After she'd dried them, she sat down on her stool so she wouldn't tower over the little girl.

Quickly, she assessed all Amanda's mostly healed bicycle crash wounds. No signs of infection and the edges of the lacerations approximated well, with no gaps or dehiscence. A few sutures were completely covered with a thin layer of skin growth because of how long they'd been in, but with care Melissa could remove them without hurting Amanda too much.

"The stitches have to come out or your knee won't heal properly." Melissa put her hand on Amanda's. "The good thing is that taking the stitches out doesn't usually hurt. Because of how long these have been in, you may feel a little pinch, but it shouldn't be too bad."

"I don't want them out." Amanda started crying loudly, more for her mother's attention than fear. "Don't let her take them out."

Melissa frowned at Amanda's behavior. She'd understood the girl's screams when she'd been sutured, but this wasn't normal behavior for Amanda.

"Amanda, they have to come out. Be good for Dr Melissa," Jamie's tired voice pleaded.

"My daddy wouldn't let her hurt me." The little girl crossed her arms, big tears rolling down her cheeks. She looked duly pitiful. "He'd never let anyone hurt me."

Unbelievably, considering how pale she already was, Jamie's face became even more ashen. "Dr Melissa isn't going to hurt you."

Melissa and Jamie both attempted to soothe Amanda, but the little girl wasn't having any of it. Melissa got Debbie to place Amanda in her lap, pinned her arms, and tucked Amanda's lower legs between hers in a big hug.

"Shh, it's going to be OK," Debbie cooed, trying to comfort the squirming but trapped child. "Dr Melissa is going to help your knee get better."

"My knee is better. Stop. Stop. Daddy!" Amanda screamed.

Melissa worked quickly to glove up and painstakingly remove each suture with her pickups and suture scissors. Only one bled and, considering how overgrown with skin they'd become, Melissa wasn't complaining.

"Almost done," she assured her unhappy and uncooperative patient.

She cleaned the wound and covered it with a large square sticky plaster.

"Debbie, could you take Amanda to the treasure chest and let her pick a prize for being so brave?"

The nurse gave her a "Brave? Yeah, right" look, but smiled sweetly at Amanda. "Let's go see if we can find you a pretty ring to match your shirt."

Amanda recovered with miraculous speed. Skipping, she followed Debbie. "I want a yo-yo."

"I'm sorry she gave you such a hard time," Jamie apologized the second they were alone. "She stays upset all the time. I can't make her happy."

"It's not your job to make her happy twenty-four hours a day, Jamie. It's OK if she gets upset from time to time. We all do. It's how we learn, grow emotionally."

Jamie's head lowered. "But I can't seem to ever make her happy. Or Cindy either."

"I know better than that."

"You don't understand." Tears streamed down Jamie's bloated face. "She told me she hates me and wishes I'd been the one to die."

"She didn't mean it, Jamie." Melissa's heart ached. "Children say things they shouldn't. I'm not excusing what she said, but she's a child and doesn't fully understand the ramifications of what she says."

"Cindy says the same thing." Thirteen was a little harder to excuse than five. "If my own kids hate me so much, what do I have to live for?"

How could Jamie's children be so cruel? They were just children, but couldn't they see how sick their mother was? How much their words hurt? No, they were kids, even Cindy at thirteen. They only saw that their mother was no longer able to jump through hoops. Hoops Jamie had done her best to leap through since their father died.

"They're confused. And scared." Melissa knew her words were the truth even if the girls' hurtful actions angered her. "Their father died and now they see you getting sick. They're afraid they might lose you, too, and they're taking out those fears on you."

Jamie gave a weak nod. "Maybe you're right, but I'm just so tired. I asked Cindy to help me, but she won't. I don't have the energy to argue with her, and she knows it. She does what she wants to."

"It's normal that she's going to test her boundaries. All kids do." Melissa squeezed Jamie's hand. "It'll be difficult, but you have to stick with what you tell the girls. If they don't do their chores, take away a favored plaything. If they argue, put them in their room."

"But they already hate me."

"No, they just need boundaries set and to know you love them."

"I do love them." Jamie shook her head, but didn't look convinced her love mattered to her girls.

"I know you do." Melissa squeezed Jamie's hand. "You're a wonderful, caring mother."

"I'm a terrible mother," the woman sobbed, tears streaming down her cheeks.

"No, you're an overwhelmed mother who is doing the best she can under the circumstances. Cindy and Amanda are dealing with emotions they're too young to understand. Honestly, they need counseling and so do you."

Jamie opened her mouth, but Melissa held up her hand.

"I know you're doing all you can to just get to your chemotherapy. Perhaps the school system can arrange for a counselor to talk to the girls. I'd love them to see a grief specialist, but whatever we can get locally will have to do for now. Until you finish your chemotherapy."

Jamie's sobs worsened and her chest shook from her tears. "See, my girls need counseling, and I can't even get them what they need. What kind of mother am I? They'd be better off without me."

"That's simply not true. No one can love Amanda and Cindy the way you do. You're their mother. They need you." Never had Melissa known Jamie to be so down, so piteous. "You will make it through this. Once you finish with the chemotherapy, you'll start to feel better."

"Once I finish with the chemotherapy, Dr Arnold is going to cut off my breast. I'm not even going to be a woman anymore."

Melissa wrapped her arms around Jamie and let the woman cry. A good cry could accomplish things that sometimes weeks of therapy didn't achieve.

When Jamie's tears slowed, she swatted at her eyes. "I'm so sorry. I shouldn't have laid all this on you. I don't know what's wrong with me. I just keep crying all the time. I don't know why."

"Honey, it's normal for you to be depressed. You were still recovering from Roger's death and coping with raising the girls by yourself. Then the cancer knocks you off your feet. What woman wouldn't be upset? Maybe we should consider a short-term antidepressant."

"Melissa?" Debbie poked her head back into the exam room. "I'm sorry to interrupt, but Cindy just threw up in the lobby. I've got her in the bathroom with a washcloth on her forehead."

Jamie's eyes glazed over with self-derision. "See, I was focused on me instead of taking care of her."

Melissa pointed at Jamie. "You stay there. Lie down on the exam table if you'd like. I'll check on Cindy and tell you what's going on after I've examined her."

Unfortunately Cindy Moss had caught the stomach virus and had been battling diarrhea most of the day without telling her mother. Jamie couldn't deal with a sick child, neither did the woman need to be exposed to the germ with her immune system weakened from her chemotherapy.

Melissa's office wasn't really set up to double as a hospital ward, but she had on occasion given intravenous fluids via an IV, and kept the supplies on hand.

When Melissa checked the teenager, she was dehydrated. Melissa convinced Jamie to leave Cindy at the office for IV fluids overnight.

Several hours, a shot of Phenergan in her hip, and a bag of normal saline later, the girl was resting in a hospital cot in one of the exam rooms.

Melissa, on the other hand, hadn't slept at all. She sat in a chair with the back of her head propped against the wall, watching over Jamie's daughter.

She'd slowed the rate of Cindy's IV fluids and the bag should last a couple of hours.

So much for that relaxing bath and a good night's sleep, she thought wryly. Not that she'd probably have slept any better than she had any other night for the past month and a half.

In the dimly lit room, she glanced at her watch. After midnight.

Her hands cradled protectively over her belly, she closed her eyes, meaning to rest them only for a few minutes.

"What the hell do you think you're doing?" an angry male voice asked.

Melissa jerked awake, her eyes popping open in startled fear. "James?"

"Yes, it's me, but it could have been anyone. The front door wasn't locked, Melissa. Anyone could have walked into this office and found you asleep."

She blinked, trying to open her tired eyes, trying to

convince herself that James towered over her, his face an angry red, chiding her for an unlocked door.

"I thought I locked it." She glanced at her watch. After two, although she'd swear she'd just shut her eyes seconds ago.

"You should have double-checked. It's not safe for you to be here at night alone with the front door unlocked for anyone to walk in."

"I'm not alone." Melissa gestured to the girl lying on the cot. As if sensing she was being talked about, Cindy made a soft moaning sound, but didn't completely rouse. "Let's go to my office so we don't wake her."

James's jaw flexed, but he didn't argue. Just watched her. Melissa ached from sitting in the chair so long, but refused to grimace under James's eagle eye.

She checked Cindy's IV line, then shuffled to her office, stretching to ease the ache in her lower back.

She needed to kill the intimacy of being in a dimly lit room with James, needed to see him, to know he was really there. She flipped on the light switch.

Although she wasn't sure she wanted James to see her.

"What the hell are you doing, Melissa?" he ground out. "That girl should be in the hospital if she needs an IV. Not here in your office with you dead on your feet."

"The hospital wasn't an option."

His eyes narrowed, and although he looked angry, his tone lowered. "No insurance?"

"She has TennCare." Tennessee's government provided insurance for the underprivileged and needy.

Confusion flickered across his handsome features. "Then why keep her here?"

Melissa inhaled a deep breath, fighting the need to rub her neck. What was he doing at her office in the middle of the night, fussing at her? And why was she letting him?

"Look, James, I don't have to explain myself to you. My patient needed fluids and I'm giving them to her. End of story."

Shaking with anger, he glared at her. "You're determined to push yourself too far, aren't you?"

"Cindy needed me."

James swore under his breath. "She needs her parents to take her to Dekalb General so she can get proper care." He glanced around her empty office. "Where are they, anyway? Shouldn't they be here?"

"Her father died last year and her mother is at home with her five-year-old sister." Melissa curled her fingers, putting her clenched hands on her hips and mentally daring James to say anything negative about Jamie. She'd likely punch him if he did.

His gaze dropped to her fists. His mouth twisted with frustration, he appeared ready to strangle her. Instead, he took a deep breath. "If you were going to keep the girl here, you should have made her mother stay to help you."

Cranky from fatigue, from being woken up, from the surprise of seeing him, and how just looking at him made her heart ache, she didn't budge from her stance. "Whether or not she should have stayed is none of your business. Just as what I do is none of your business."

He looked taken aback, like she'd slapped him. What did he think? That he could run roughshod over her life, but she had no say in his world? Hardly.

Yet she hated the disillusionment in his eyes.

Frustration washed over Melissa. She didn't want to argue with him. Didn't really have the energy to do so, although she'd never admit that to him.

"James, I know you're trying to help," she sighed, "but Cindy is my patient. I'm doing what I believe is best for her and her family."

"What about what's best for you and your family? Is working yourself to the bone, not getting any rest—is that what's best for you? For our baby?"

"I…" Melissa stopped, unable to go on. James was right. She glanced up, ready to concede his point.

The anger on his face melted into concern, and he raked his fingers through his hair. Hair that, she noticed, had been trimmed to its normal neat style since her ultrasound.

Two in the morning and he looked fabulous in his navy scrubs. Like he'd walked straight off some television show about doctors. Like he was the sexy star that made women tune in week after week for another drool-worthy episode.

"Go." He motioned to the comfy leather sofa that was pushed up against her office wall. "Lie down and sleep."

"I can't." She shook her head. "Cindy."

He sighed. "I'll keep an eye on her. You sleep."

She wanted to argue, but fatigue and the steely look in his eyes held her tongue. "You're sure?"

"Positive." His tone softened. "One of us has to look out for our child and you're too stubborn to take care of yourself, much less our baby. Get some rest, even if it's just a short nap. I'll watch over the girl."

A short nap. Just a few more minutes of sleep.

Because she was sleepy. Exhausted. When she'd rested a bit, she'd tell him that she was taking care of their baby, taking her vitamins, and forcing down three meals a day.

"I'm not that tired." Melissa yawned, giving herself away.

"Lie down," he ordered. "Now, before I make you."

Under different circumstances James making her to lie down could have been a fun experience. Now he was too reserved, too serious, too not hers anymore.

Just a short nap. That's all she needed. Then she'd have the energy to deal with him.

She lay down on the sofa and covered herself with the afghan Norma Prater had crocheted after Melissa diagnosed her granddaughter's appendicitis mere hours before the appendix would have ruptured. Melissa had arranged for Dr Arnold to see the girl that same morning and he'd done an emergency appendectomy just in the nick of time.

According to Norma, Dr Arnold had said the girl would have died, or at least been critically ill, if Melissa hadn't acted so quickly.

She loved her job. Taking care of others came naturally, made her feel alive, gave her purpose, and made her feel needed.

James was right when he'd said she needed to be needed. She did. Perhaps it came from feeling like an unwanted fifth wheel during her childhood.

Treating her like a kid, James tucked the blanket Norma had made with love around her. His touch firm, yet gentle. Easily, she could picture him doing the same for their baby.

James would be a good father.

She hugged the blanket to her, letting its softness wrap her in coziness. Or maybe the coziness came from knowing James stood close.

"Cindy's chart is on my desk if you need it." She yawned again, her insides feeling warmer than they had in weeks. "You'll wake me if she needs me?"

Watching her curl up on the sofa, he nodded. "I'm sure she'll be fine. Good night, Melissa."

Melissa closed her eyes. "Good night, James."

CHAPTER SEVEN

MELISSA became aware of her surroundings in slow steps. The first thing to strike her was the pain in her lower back.

She went to stretch and realized she wasn't in her bed at her house. She was on the sofa in her office.

James was there, looking after Cindy.

She opened her eyes, squinted to make out her watch hands. Ten o'clock? No way.

Ignoring her protesting muscles, she sat up.

Why hadn't James woken her up?

She glanced at the drawn window shades. Shades she always kept open. The sunlight would have woken her. Which probably answered her question of why he'd drawn them to begin with.

Now she would be more behind than ever.

Dizziness washed over her the moment she stood up. When was this horrible sick feeling ever going to pass?

She made the necessary trip to the private bathroom in her office. After she finished business and brushing her teeth, she splashed water on her face.

She'd slept better than she had in weeks. But now she

had patients who'd been waiting all morning. Plus, Cindy's IV would need to be changed.

James would be long gone as he had classes today. Why had he made the drive last night? Arrived at her office in the dead of night? Put her to bed, well, sofa?

Or had she been so exhausted she'd dreamed the whole thing?

No, if she'd been dreaming, James would have taken her into his arms and begged her to forgive his stupidity for leaving and her stupidity for letting him go, and of course he'd want their baby. Yeah, that was definitely dream stuff.

Last night he'd been angry.

Except she'd swear she remembered him brushing her hair away from her face right as she'd drifted off to sleep. That his warm lips had brushed her temple and he'd mumbled something under his breath.

She'd likely dreamed the whole thing.

She changed into fresh scrubs, pulled her hair back in a neat ponytail, and went to face the drama of having overslept on a busy Thursday morning.

She immediately bumped into Debbie. The nurse averted her gaze and seemed to be hiding a smile. A guilty smile.

"Why didn't you wake me?"

Still not making eye contact, Debbie threw her hands up. "Hey, I had strict orders that you were not to be disturbed, no matter what."

Strict orders? "From who?"

"The tooth fairy." Debbie quipped. "Who do you think?"

"James?"

"James."

James had been there and stuck around until Debbie had arrived. Which meant she hadn't dreamed last night. He had kissed her forehead. Why? And what was it he'd said? Even fully awake, she couldn't decipher his mumbled words.

"What's that smile for?" Debbie smirked and Melissa instantly flattened her expression.

"Nothing," she assured her. What was she thinking, smiling in front of Debbie? Her friend would gnaw on that like a dog on a bone.

"Yeah, right." Debbie's brown eyes rolled toward the ceiling.

Melissa started to respond, then remembered Cindy. "How's Cindy this morning? I should go check her. Did James change her IV bag before leaving this morning?"

"Her bag is changed, and she's much better." James spoke from behind her, causing Melissa to spin toward him. She almost lost her balance, but recovered so quickly she didn't think anyone noticed her lapse.

"I'm going to discharge her home," James continued.

Discharge her? Was he making fun that she'd treated her office like a hospital?

Melissa eyed him suspiciously. "I thought you'd left."

"I heard," he commented dryly, his gaze traveling over her in a slow perusal.

She fought the need to fidget under his assessing stare. What was he planning to do, write a thesis on her midmorning appearance?

"I've got the urinalysis back on John Brown." Debbie

waved the chart she held, reminding them that she was there and privy to their conversation.

"Thanks, Debbie," Melissa automatically replied, wondering what was wrong with John Brown.

"I think she was talking to me." James smiled wryly, taking the chart and flipping to the lab section.

Melissa's mouth dropped. Her nurse just gave a shrug and, suppressing a smile, returned to the nurses' station.

"You've been seeing my patients?"

"Yes," he answered, so nonchalantly one could almost believe it was no big deal. She knew better.

"I'm not sure my malpractice insurance covers you." Why she said something so corny she didn't know, but the prickly words came out of her mouth.

His lips twisted. "You may recall that I have my own malpractice insurance."

Unsure what to say and not wanting to come out with something as inane as before, Melissa glanced around the hallway. Her gaze landed on a diabetes poster. She focused on the diagram of the pancreas without really seeing the insulin-producing organ.

"Don't you have class today?" she asked, when the silence had dragged on too long.

He nodded. "I teach on Tuesdays and Thursdays."

"Then why are you here?"

"I asked a friend to cover my class this morning."

"Why?" She asked the obvious question.

He shrugged, again playing nonchalance to the max. "Because there are more important things than my work."

An answer that could have a thousand meanings and each and every one ran through Melissa's befuddled head. He'd come because she'd needed him. Somehow he'd known.

Although she would have made it with Cindy, having James there eased the strain on her body. Despite her initial stiffness, she felt better than she had in weeks.

He closed the chart and glanced away, seeming to think about what he wanted to say before speaking. "Look, I've got things under control. Go home, take a shower, read a book, whatever you want to do. Just rest."

Go home? Was he joking? "I can't."

"Didn't you hear me? You can. I'll take care of everything here."

"You can't."

His brow lifted. "Are you saying you're a better doctor than I am?"

Melissa opened her mouth, then closed it. What could she say? That she thought she cared for her patients more than he did? That he treated the medical problem rather than the person as a whole? That he remained too detached to provide what her patients needed?

"Go back to Nashville, James. I'm not leaving my patients."

He swore loud enough and with enough fury that Melissa was surprised no one came to check on her. He spun round, paced across the hall, turned, and met her gaze. Steely determination shone in his blue eyes. "I'm staying."

His entire demeanor said nothing she did would make him budge.

"Fine." She glanced at the chart in his hands, tugged it free. "Suit yourself. I'm going to check on John Brown."

His jaw flexing, James took the chart from her before she'd even taken two steps. "Mr Brown is expecting *me* to finish seeing him. Go find your own patient."

Knowing James was in the same building was driving Melissa crazy. Almost noon and she'd only seen a handful of patients. James had breezed through the morning, seeing patient after patient with a speed that drove her bonkers. How could he be meeting their needs when he barely spent any time with them? It wasn't like he knew anything about them. Things like John Brown's brother was diagnosed with prostate cancer a month ago and that John worried his prostate was a ticking time bomb.

With each passing minute her antagonism toward James grew. She admitted her anger bordered on the ir-rational, but she wanted to lash out at him and knew before the day ended they'd have words.

"Melissa?" Debbie interrupted her thoughts.

Melissa glanced up from the chart she was writing in and glared at her traitorous friend.

"I hate to bother you, but James's doing a department of transportation physical on Luke Robison." Debbie ignored the visual daggers zooming her way. "I just put Bob Woods in room two. His stomach is hurting, and he says it's pretty bad. I've got a urinalysis and a complete blood count going on him. Do you want any other tests?"

"Let me check him first. I'll be right there." She put her pen in her scrubs pocket, then leered at her nurse. "Unless you'd rather wait on James?"

"Well, if he hadn't just started," Debbie mused, with

sarcasm only a real friend could get away with, "I would. You'll have to do."

"Hi, Bob, what's going on?" Melissa asked the fifty-nine-year-old when she entered the exam room.

Bob paced back and forth. "Something bad, Doc. My insides feel like Dana Higgins's mule trampled them."

"When did the pain start?"

"I hurt a little last night, but this morning the pain done gone and got bad on me."

"Have you seen any blood in your urine?"

"Ain't paid no attention to that, Doc."

"Any diarrhea or constipation?"

"I'm like clockwork after dinner."

Melissa asked a few more questions, made notes in the chart. "Have a seat," she told the still pacing man, "and I'll check you."

Having him take off his shirt first, which he did with several grunts and moans, she listened to Bob's heart and lungs. Nothing abnormal. She motioned for him to lie back on the table, and for a moment she didn't think he was going to comply, but, grimacing, he slowly lowered himself.

"Show me where you hurt," she ordered. He pointed to his right lower quadrant, close to the midline. "That's an appendectomy scar, isn't it?"

"Had my appendix out when I was fourteen," he confirmed.

"Have you ever had a kidney stone?" From the amount of pain he was in, she suspected that might be the culprit.

"A few years ago. You think this is another one?"

He winced. "I hurt up higher with the last one. More in my back."

Melissa listened to his abdomen, but everything sounded normal. She went to lightly palpate it, but Bob's hand covered hers.

"I don't think I can let you do that."

"I have to check you. I'll be as gentle as I can."

Swallowing, Bob nodded, closed his eyes and visibly braced himself for expected pain. Melissa's sense of unease grew.

She gently checked him, but his guarding prevented her from feeling confident in her exam.

"Bob, I'm going to do an X-ray of your abdomen as I can run that here at the office. Depending on that and what the tests Debbie ran show, I will likely send you to Dekalb General for a CT scan of your abdomen and pelvis."

Melissa stepped out of the room and went into the small lab where Debbie and the lab technician stood.

"He's got four plus blood in his urine. Think it's a kidney stone?" Debbie asked.

"His blood count is normal," Stacey, the lab technician, who was also certified as an X-ray technician, said. "And everything else on his urinalysis is normal."

Which would make one think Bob had a kidney stone.

"I'd like an abdominal and pelvic X-ray. Maybe the stone will show. Come get me when it's done."

Melissa went back to her desk to do some paperwork while she waited.

A few minutes later Debbie stuck her head in the doorway. "X-ray's ready. He has a stone on the right."

Relief washed over Melissa. She would order some

strong pain medication for Bob, have him drink plenty of fluids, and send him for a CT scan this afternoon.

But when she looked at the X-ray, she frowned. The stone was too high. Other than a lot of gas in the intestines, probably from his pain, she didn't see anything else abnormal.

"I'm finished with my last patient for the morning." James walked up behind her to look over her shoulder at the X-ray light box. "Debbie said you needed help."

"She lied."

"Admit it. This morning went a lot smoother with me here."

"I'd have managed." She refused to admit anything. She stared at Bob's X-ray, trying to ignore the man behind her. Difficult to do when her five senses went into overdrive at his nearness.

"No doubt. No matter if it compromises your health. Or our baby's."

"Our baby is fine."

"For the moment, but you're determined to do everything you can to change that, aren't you?"

She spun, glared at him. "You have no right to come in here and say anything to me." She spat the words out, shaking with emotion. "I didn't get pregnant on purpose, but I want our baby and am glad I'm pregnant. You're the one who's probably hoping I'll miscarry so you won't have to deal with a baby and can be done with me for good."

She winced the moment the words left her mouth. She knew they weren't true, that James would never wish her to miscarry, regardless of how he felt about having a baby. Feelings that she felt certain had softened on the day of her ultrasound.

He paled, grabbed her arms, and pulled her to him. Never had she felt such anger course through him, seen his eyes darken to the stormy shade of blue glaring at her. And the worst part was that she deserved his anger.

Debbie poked her head into the room. "Bob is asking for you, Melissa. His pain is worse."

Oh, God. How could she have forgotten she still had a patient? A very sick one at that.

James's hold on her arm tightened. "We're not finished."

"It'll have to wait."

"I grew tired of waiting for you months ago."

Her gaze shot to his. "Fine. Let me go."

His lips thinned to a white line, but his fingers loosened. "Go, but I'm not leaving. We're going to finish this conversation."

Melissa ran from the room and into Bob's exam room. Sure enough, he was doubled over. His forehead glistened with sweat, and he held his abdomen much lower than where the stone resided.

Referred pain? Some people did experience pain in places other than where the actual problem was, but her gut instinct said that wasn't the case.

"The pain's worse?"

"I'm dying."

Melissa made a fast decision. She couldn't convince herself that a kidney stone was causing his pain. "I'm going to call for an ambulance to take you to Dekalb. I'll send you through the emergency room for testing."

She expected the older man to argue, but he nodded, further upping her suspicions. She turned, planning to call for the ambulance, and practically bumped into James, who carried the X-ray film.

"Melissa, take another look at this. There's a shadow. I'm not sure it's anything, but have a look." James held the film up, letting the ceiling light illuminate the film. "Right there."

A shadow? She looked closely at the area he indicated near the distal portion of the abdominal aorta, close to where the right iliac artery branched. Very subtle, but there could be a shadow. Or it could be incidental.

"I'm sending him to Dekalb by ambulance."

In full doctor mode, James nodded. "Good idea. It's exactly what I was thinking."

She rushed out to make the call. When she stepped back into the exam room, she saw James gently talking to Bob. The older man had a ghastly hue to his dark skin.

"They're on their way."

A loud pop had Bob crying out, grabbing his stomach. James and Melissa's eyes met. A chill ran over her spine. Oh, God. There had been a shadow.

An aortic aneurysm shadow. A weakness in the vascular wall of the largest blood vessel in the body that caused a bulge. That bulge had just ruptured.

"We need to start an IV, stat," James ordered. Kicking immediately into the role he played best, he helped Bob lie back on the table and propped his feet up.

Her adrenaline jolting, Melissa gathered what she'd need, calling for Debbie so she could send her for anything else that she and James might think of.

"Call Life Flight," she told the nurse. "We need a helicopter, stat. Bob Woods just popped an aortic aneurysm."

"Isn't that fatal?" Debbie asked, her eyes wide while she watched Melissa grab a bag of normal saline IV fluid and an IV line.

"Almost always," Melissa responded, hating it that statistics said Bob Woods wouldn't live to see another day.

Within seconds she inserted the needle and was attaching the bag of fluid.

"Give it wide open," James ordered. "We've got to keep enough fluid in him to keep his vital organs profused."

Bob mumbled something, but his eyes were closed.

"Did you give something to sedate him?"

James shook his head. "He's gone into shock and his body is cutting off all non-essential functions to conserve energy. Hold his legs completely up."

Side by side, they did what little could be done until Life Flight arrived.

The moment she heard the buzz of the helicopter, Melissa sighed. Despite their efforts, Bob's vitals were rapidly dropping as the ruptured aneurysm bled into his abdominal cavity. Actually, his pulse holding as well as it was amazed her. Bob Woods was bleeding to death on the inside.

"They're taking him to Vanderbilt," James told her when the helicopter was in the air. "I've called and spoken with the emergency room staff. He'll be taken straight into the operating room on arrival."

Relief washing over her that everything that could be done to save Bob's life would be done, she nodded.

A small crowd had gathered in Melissa's parking lot. Emergency airlifts rarely occurred in Sawtooth, usually from motor vehicle accidents when they did, but never from Melissa's office.

Her hands shook, her knees wobbled, and her stomach churned, but she forced a smile at the curious onlookers. Debbie was already rushing them back to their business.

A hot flush coated Melissa's skin with moisture and her eyes dimmed. She needed to sit down. Now.

So she did. Right there in the middle of the parking lot. Still, she fought to keep conscious, so she lowered her head to between her knees. At least, as much as her belly would allow.

"Melissa?" both James and Debbie called. Their voices sounded far away, but she could feel them touching her.

"I'm fine." But she wasn't. The stress of the night before, of fighting with James, with knowing she might never hear Bob's laughter or see him peddling his hand-made rocking chairs ever again, had caught up with her.

"Isn't this exactly what I've been saying was going to happen?" James swore, scooped Melissa into his arms, and headed into the building. "You are going to make some changes if I have to kidnap you and force you to."

"Debbie heard you threaten me," she warned, wishing his arms didn't feel so good around her, wishing his spicy male scent didn't fill her with lust. Lust! How could she feel desire at a time like this?

"Debbie is so worried about you that she'd pack your bag and wish me luck."

Melissa closed her eyes, hating her weakness. Her physical weakness that had caused her to sit down in the middle of her parking lot. Her emotional weakness that jumped excitedly at the prospect of him taking her far away, just the two of them somewhere peaceful and stress-free.

"What? No argument?" he asked, as he laid her on the sofa in her office, but she immediately sat up.

Missing his body warmth, Melissa rubbed her bare arms. "I'm OK now. I just got a little light-headed."

"No."

"No?" She raised a brow, not understanding what he meant.

"No, you aren't going to shove aside the hints your body is giving that you need to slow down."

"James, lots of women get light-headed during pregnancy."

"We're not talking about lots of women. We're talking about you. You and our baby." The angry spark was back in his eyes. "Despite what you obviously think, the last thing I want is for you to miscarry. Although you're giving a damned good impression that it's what you want and I have to wonder why. Are you pushing yourself out of guilt?"

She reeled back, not believing what he was saying. "No," she gasped.

"Then stop acting in ways that give the impression this baby means nothing to you."

"How dare you?"

"Furthermore," he said, ignoring her outburst, "you have to start thinking about the future. You can't work like this after the baby arrives. At least for the first few weeks, you're going to need to regain your strength. Who's going to take care of your precious patients while you do that?"

"Haven't you heard of the women who gave birth and went straight back to picking cotton?" she asked flippantly.

"Perhaps you might recall just how short those women's lifespans were."

Ouch.

"You think you have all the answers," she accused, knowing that whether or not she felt up to another row, there was going to be one. "Well, you don't. What am I supposed to do? Just let people die? That's not who I am, James. I don't turn my back on people."

"You turned your back on me," he said angrily. "On us."

"You're the one who walked when you found out I was pregnant," she reminded him.

"Your pregnancy had little to do with the reasons I left. You turned your back on me months before that. My leaving just brought it to your attention."

"You ran away," she accused, pulling Norma's Afghan to her protectively.

"I wanted to wake you up to the fact that you put every single person's needs in front of mine. You killed our relationship." He leaned in, his face inches from hers. "I want to know why."

She pushed against his chest. "Because I wanted a baby and every time I looked at you, all I could think was that I'd never have a real family if we stayed together."

CHAPTER EIGHT

JAMES stared at Melissa's ashen face and couldn't believe what she'd just admitted. Despite having been honest, having told her he didn't want kids, she'd wanted a baby all along. If she weren't such an ethical person, he'd suspect her of having intentionally gotten pregnant.

Her surprised, guilty-appearing face said she was just as shocked at her admission as he was. If having a family had meant so much to her, why had she agreed to no kids?

His gaze lowered to her swollen belly. "It looks like you get what you want."

She grimaced. "Like this wasn't what I wanted."

"Regardless, you are pregnant. For the sake of our baby, we're going to make changes to our current arrangement."

"What kind of changes?" she asked suspiciously. "I've already told you that I'm not going to sell my practice."

"I think we both know that your practice is your number one priority, so that's out." His statement sounded more like a slur even to his own ears.

"That's not fair."

"No," he agreed, "but, then, no one said life had to be fair. I should move back in."

"What about…?" She stopped, her face screwing up unpleasantly. "Nashville?"

"I'm going to ask for a leave of absence until after the baby is born."

"From the hospital?" she asked, not bothering to hide her shock.

"Yes."

"What about your classes? Your research?"

"I'll continue." He shrugged. "Two mornings a week and I'll spend those afternoons in the lab."

"I admitted weeks ago that I wanted you to come home and you refused. Why now?"

"Don't take my moving back wrong. It's for selfish reasons."

"What selfish reasons?"

"I want my baby to have every advantage. Being healthy seems an important one. You forget or are too busy to take care of your needs, things like sleep, good nutrition, keeping your stress to a minimum, thus unintentionally hurting our baby."

"You arrogant…" Again she stopped, searching for a vile enough word.

"Probably," he agreed to whatever name she planned to call him. "But I'm moving back so I can look out for our child. But you've got to make concessions, too, Melissa. No more late nights. I'll help with the calls that can't be diverted to Dekalb, but you have to start cutting the community's dependency on you. You can't do it all."

She opened her mouth to deny him, but he'd had enough.

"I'll keep your practice going so that after the baby is born you can step back in and not miss a beat—if that's what you want. In return, you're going to take care of yourself and my baby." He stared into her eyes, knowing he wouldn't back down on this. Not after last night and this afternoon. Neither would he take no for an answer. "If this baby means anything to you, you'll meet me halfway. Now, tell me what you want for lunch, and I'll feed you. Then you're going home to rest and think about everything I've said. I'll see your afternoon patients and bring our dinner home with me, so don't bother fixing anything."

That evening, Melissa lounged on her living-room sofa and reread the same sentence for at least the hundredth time. Although she loved reading, her heart just wasn't into it. Or into anything except checking the clock on the fireplace mantel. Two minutes since the last time she'd checked.

After six and no sign of James.

Maybe she should call Debbie again, make sure James truly had everything under control.

What was she thinking? Of course he did. He was a highly sought-after Vanderbilt emergency room physician.

One that she'd always admired. Well, until that night when she'd watched him with Lila Barnes and become disenchanted.

Which really wasn't fair.

She'd been upset, tired, frustrated, disenchanted long before she'd walked into that waiting room and judged him through the eyes of anger and disillusionment.

Just as she'd been subconsciously angry at him for months. She hadn't realized how angry until that afternoon when they'd argued and she'd admitted the truth. She'd resented him for denying her what she'd craved her whole life—a family. And now she was essentially doing the same to him, forcing a family on him when it wasn't what he wanted.

How could she want him in her life, want his baby, and steal his dreams in the process? Was he right? Had she been pushing herself so hard after discovering her pregnancy because of guilt? She'd thought she worked so hard to avoid her loneliness and loss at James's absence, but she did feel guilty. Why did her dream have to be in direct conflict with what he wanted? And although seeing the ultrasound had softened his heart, that didn't mean he'd have chosen parenthood.

Headlights appeared in the drive, flickering light through the large windows along the front of the house. The garage door ground open. James was home.

Melissa set down her book, and stood. What was she doing? Running to the door to greet him? Just because she planned to agree to his terms, it didn't mean a thing had changed between them. They were two people torn apart but bound by a baby.

She sat, picked up the book, and pretended to read. Pretended because the words blurred and her heart thudded while she strained for the sound of James's car pulling into the garage, of his car door opening and closing, of him entering the house.

And then there he was. Opening the kitchen door and walking through the house, sinking onto the opposite end of the sofa, looking handsome, as always, but exhausted.

He leaned back, his deep blue eyes watching her through shaded lids. She fought squirming.

"How did it go today?" she asked, rather than admit how strongly he threw her off-kilter.

"Fine."

"Any word on Bob Woods?"

"I called and checked on him on my way home. He's still in surgery and it's touch-and-go, but for the time being he's holding his own. Fortunately, he was bleeding into an area of the abdominal cavity that, when it filled with blood, helped put pressure on the ruptured aneurysm, which slowed the blood loss. Otherwise he wouldn't have had a chance of surviving."

She nodded, her stomach twisting once again at what would have happened had James not been at the office. Silence loomed again and Melissa could feel his eyes watching her.

"Cindy Moss? How's she?" She really should have talked to Jamie today, seen how the young woman was holding up. Instead, she'd gone home after lunch and soaked in a tub of lukewarm water, yearning for hot water but knowing it wasn't recommended during pregnancy. She'd left the office prior to Jamie returning from her chemo.

"Back to normal."

"That's good to hear." They sounded pathetic, like strangers making small talk.

"I met her mother today."

"Jamie?" she asked, wondering why she sounded so surprised. James would have met her when she'd picked up Cindy. "How's she?"

"Not nearly as well as her daughter."

Melissa could believe that. Jamie didn't have the resources to cope well with the problems she faced.

"We talked for a long time. She told me everything you've done."

Heat burned Melissa's cheeks. "Just doing my job."

"No." He brushed his palms down his thighs, looking pensive. "You've done much more than that, much more than most doctors would have, and we both know it."

He sounded so sincere, so full of praise rather than condemnation that Melissa found it hard to swallow.

"One day of working at the clinic and your disposition about my patients has totally changed?" She regarded him suspiciously. "I don't buy it."

"My disposition hasn't changed." He didn't bat an eyelash. "I think you work too hard and too much."

"Did my small-town practice bore you to tears?" Another one of those moments when she wondered why she hadn't held her tongue. They were having a decent enough conversation. Why purposely bait him?

"You'd ask me that after airlifting a ruptured aortic aneurysm?" he snorted, then gave a slow smile. "Surprisingly, even beyond Bob Woods, it didn't."

Surprising indeed.

"Why did you get someone to cover for you today?"

James's smile faded and his eyes narrowed. He considered her for a long time. "I got my class covered because when you didn't answer my calls last night, I got worried."

"And drove to Sawtooth in the middle of the night?"

"I kept trying here and your cell phone. It was when I still couldn't get you after midnight that I got worried, arranged for someone to cover the rest of my ER shift."

"You were working last night?"

He nodded. "Why didn't you answer your cell phone? I know you keep that thing on you at all times."

Usually she did keep the phone near her, but she hated carrying it because of possible radiation to the baby. There was too much controversy on the subject to take a chance. She'd gotten into the habit of leaving it on her desk.

"I turned it to vibrate so it wouldn't wake Cindy, then didn't hear it vibrating when you called."

"You scared me."

By the dark look in his eyes, she could tell he had feared for her safety. "I'd have called if something happened, James."

"If you could call."

She gave a nervous laugh. "Don't be so melodramatic. I'm fine. I was fine last night."

"There was nothing fine about you last night. You were exhausted and risking your health, our baby's health, and that of your patient."

"My patient is fine. You said so yourself."

"Even before you were pregnant, you'd forget to eat. Many a night I think you would have forgone eating altogether if I hadn't already had you something ready."

"That's in the past. Since my pregnancy test, I've made myself eat three times a day even when I'm so nauseated I can barely stomach a cracker."

"Good for you, but you still look awful."

"Thanks," she snorted.

"Sometimes the truth hurts."

"Like the truth that you left me for Dr Weaver?" Why had she said that? She knew he hadn't left her for the cardiologist. Jealousy, pure and simple in its ugly, green-eyed form.

"I didn't leave you for Kristen," he immediately denied. "Kristen is my friend, nothing more, and never will be. I left because you failed to value our relationship, weren't willing to give what I needed."

Wasn't that why she'd pushed him away, too? Because he wouldn't give her what she wanted? A baby.

But he had given her one. Unintentionally, but his baby was growing within her belly all the same.

"I valued our relationship." And how did he know what she hadn't been willing to give? Was he referring to his asinine suggestion that she sell her practice and move to Nashville?

"Really? From where I'm sitting, it didn't appear so. I asked you to give me one night and you couldn't even manage that."

Guilt flooded through her, but given the same set of circumstances she'd make the same choices if she had to do it over again, even knowing that she'd come home to an empty house.

"I wanted that night to be special, James." Her eyes blurred as memories assailed her—her excitement over the way she'd looked, the silky dress that she'd ended up throwing away because of the bloodstains she'd been unable to remove. "I had my makeup and hair done, bought a new dress, but then I got a call that a little girl had come into the office and—"

"And you had to go to her rescue," he finished for her.

Melissa nodded.

"It's not that I don't admire what you do," he began. "You're a wonderful and caring doctor. It's just that you're a wonderful and caring doctor to the exclusion of all else. Nothing and no one comes before your patients. If that's the life you want, then that's your choice. I love medicine, but I want a life, too."

"You're being overly dramatic, James. I have a life." Not recently, but she had had a life until he'd walked away.

"Really?" He looked genuinely curious. "Tell me about your life, Melissa. What do you do outside medicine?"

"Lots." But she couldn't think of a single thing at the moment. But wasn't it natural that she'd bury herself in work? Anything to distract herself from the fact that only an empty house waited for her?

"When we first got together you took time to go to medical meetings with me. We'd travel to conferences, go canoeing, bicycling, or just sit on the sofa, watching a movie and eating popcorn." He closed his eyes, memories playing across his features. "How long has it been since we've spent any real time together?"

Finally a question she knew the answer to. "We went out to eat the night before my ultrasound," she reminded him.

"Not that our strained dinner counts, but I'm talking about prior to my moving back to Nashville."

She thought over the weeks before that horrible night when Ray Barnes died and, in grief, his wife overdosed.

"The day we worked in the yard, planting flowers and clearing away winter debris. We spent the entire day together."

The night, too. It was the last time she recalled making love with him other than quick sex during the night to satisfy physical need.

"That was in April. It's almost October."

She thought harder, then realized if she had to think that hard, he'd proved his point.

Why hadn't she made love to him every second he had been in her life? Kissed him and told him how wonderful it was to wake up next to him? She'd been blind.

"We weren't spending enough time together," she admitted.

"No," he agreed. "We weren't."

Why was it so much easier to see the truth in hindsight?

She took a deep breath and asked what her heart yearned to know, what she'd hoped all day his arrival at the clinic during the night meant. "Is there any way things can go back to the way they were?"

After all, he had suggested moving back in.

He stared at her for the longest time, as if he were trying to get inside her head. Melissa's hope rose. Was it possible that they could return to the life they'd shared together?

"No, there's not," James said, his voice confident, sure of his answer.

Melissa tried not to flinch, but knew she did.

His words hurt. Sharp, stabbing hurt. A fresh rejection to go with the slew of past ones. Why had she foolishly gotten her hopes up? He was here for the baby, not her.

"I don't want that life back," he continued. More pain. "Neither can we go on with the way things currently are." His weariness seeping through, he sighed. "I'm not going to go through what I did last night when I couldn't reach you. Not ever again."

"I'm sorry, James. I didn't mean to worry you. I was so worried about Cindy that I never thought about you calling."

His lips flattened into a thin line, and she realized she'd only reinforced his perception that she put her patients first, before him.

She'd never thought so. Had anyone asked, she'd have said James was the most important person in her life. So why had it been so easy to push him aside any time someone else needed her?

So easy she hadn't even realized she'd been doing it.

Not until he'd left. She wanted him back.

Had she wanted his baby that much? Yes, but their problems had run deeper than that.

"I'm willing to accept your terms." She stared straight into his eyes. "You were right about me being exhausted last night. I'd been dreaming of a soak in the tub and a good night's sleep all afternoon."

He seemed taken aback at her admission.

"I've been trying to take care of myself, but I get tired so easily," she confessed. "I saw a need in Cindy, and I did what I could to take care of it. If you hadn't arrived…" she winced at the stark truth "…I wouldn't have lasted the night."

"You would have pushed yourself and done so, Melissa. You always do."

"Maybe."

Another long silence. "If you're serious about meeting me halfway, I'll move my things back this weekend."

She didn't point out that he'd only taken his clothes when he'd left and, technically, he'd bought a lot of the furniture and household goods.

She wanted James back in her house, her life, her heart, but not against his will.

"James, you can't just put your entire life on hold like this."

"Your pregnancy has put your life on hold. I'm half-responsible for that. It only makes sense that we'd both make compromises to accommodate the baby. I plan to be an active part of our baby's life."

His face was pinched, as if the thought pained him.

"Why don't you want kids, James?"

His blue gaze shot to hers. "Under the circumstances, that's irrelevant."

"No." She shook her head, seeing fear in his eyes. Fear she didn't understand and that had nothing to do with the reasons he'd given her in the past. "For this to work, we have to be honest with each other. I've told you the truth, about having lied to you about not wanting a baby." She closed her eyes, swallowed. She placed her palms protectively over her belly. "Tell me the truth, James. Why didn't you want me to have your baby?"

"Why did you agree, Melissa?"

"Because I wasn't willing to give you up," she admitted, not wanting to but knowing one of them had to start tearing the walls down. "I hoped you'd change your mind and when you didn't, I grew to resent you."

His face harsh, he sighed. "It wasn't personal, Melissa. I don't want a baby with anyone." His gaze dropped to where she cradled her belly and he winced. "I—I—"

"Don't," she interrupted. "Don't make up something about wanting this baby, James. Tell me the truth because I know something happened somewhere along the way that's made you feel this way. What was it? Did you get some girl pregnant during high school? Is that it?"

It's what she'd always wondered in the back of her mind, but she couldn't believe she'd found the strength to give words to her thoughts.

"If only."

The bitter sadness in those two words squeezed her heart at whatever burden he carried. "Please, tell me so I can understand," she pleaded.

"I can't."

"Can't or won't?"

"There's no point in this, Melissa. We should be deciding on things like custody and where the baby is going to go to school, holidays, that kind of thing. The past doesn't matter."

This brought the custody issue to the forefront of Melissa's mind once again. Besides, he wasn't going to tell her his reasons. She bit her lower lip, battling her frustration that he still hid behind that wall, refused to let her inside, battling very real rising panic.

Not once during her dreams of wanting James's baby had she ever envisioned her child not being with her during the holidays, during every day.

"I plan to breastfeed," she warned him, just so he'd know it would be months and months before the baby would be able to be away from her for any extended amount of time.

"Good." He didn't seem bothered by her announcement, but that might have been from relief that she'd let her questioning go. "It's what's best for the baby, but I have to admit that I'm surprised."

"Why?"

"Because it'll tie you down more. You'll have to be the one to do the feeds. The baby will need to be with you."

"So you agree that it's best for the baby to stay with me until he or she is weaned?"

He took a long time answering. "I agree that we still have to figure out custody. I've talked with a lawyer and she says—"

Melissa's breath caught. "Wait a minute." All thoughts of James's past disappearing, she threw her hands up to stop him, to try to get a handle on what he'd said. "You've talked to a lawyer?"

He looked uncomfortable. "Last week."

Last week. They'd talked on the phone how many nights since then? "You didn't say anything. We've talked every night and not once have you mentioned seeing a lawyer."

"I didn't think custody an appropriate topic to

discuss over the phone. Some things should be done in person."

Still, the fact that he'd seen a lawyer made the possibility of him fighting for their child all the more real.

What was she thinking? Of course, James would fight for custody. Hadn't she known that from the moment she'd seen the tenderness in his eyes when he'd watched the ultrasound monitor?

"For the record, I understand that our baby will need you more than me during the first few months while you're nursing."

Understanding of him, she seethed. How could he have talked with a lawyer and not told her?

"I'm going to nurse until—" the kid goes to college, she thought "—I feel it's the right time to wean."

He nodded, eyeing her suspiciously, and she wondered if he'd read her mind. "I'm sure there's a lot about parenting we both need to learn."

She bit the inside of her lip, hating the strained atmosphere between them. Hating even more that she'd played a huge role in causing that strain and now she stood to lose not only him but possibly their baby.

And he hadn't even wanted a baby.

"What did your lawyer say?"

Looking tired, he sighed. "Are you sure you want to talk about this tonight?"

"Yes." She should hire a lawyer, too. Then her lawyer could talk to his lawyer and two strangers could negotiate the fate of their baby. She hated it.

"That I'm a decent, upstanding citizen with a good job and have the means and desire to provide for a child." He met her gaze, probably so she would see the honesty in his eyes. "If we fought over custody, she thinks I have a good chance of winning."

"No," Melissa gasped, placing her hand over her mouth. "I wouldn't let you take my baby."

"*Our* baby, and we've been through this. Our baby needs a mother and a father. I'm interested in joint custody, not full." He averted his gaze, then shifted it back to her, his eyes dark and full of warning. "That is, unless you become neglectful."

Which said it all. Why he'd shown up last night. Why he sat on her sofa now. James didn't trust her with their baby.

If she didn't meet his standards, he'd try to take away their baby.

"Is that what this is about? You want to move back in to spy on me? Build up information you can use as evidence later on?"

"I've already told you." He stood, glared down at her. His face flushed an angry red. "My moving back in has to do with trying to keep you from harming our baby with your lack of consideration for how your actions affect it."

CHAPTER NINE

JAMES couldn't believe they were arguing again. It wasn't what he'd wanted or planned, but maybe he'd been willing to do anything to get Melissa off his past.

Still, he'd decided to move back to Sawtooth to make her life easier. Not to argue. Why did she have to push his buttons and back him into corners where he came out verbally punching?

He hated fighting. Always had. Not that he and Melissa had ever fought much. They hadn't, which might be part of the problem. Nothing to shake them out of the status quo. These days, things shook. Hell, earthquakes couldn't jar him the way just being in the same room with Melissa did.

"Leave," she spat, standing and glaring at him with what appeared akin to hatred. "Get out of my house and don't you dare come back."

James closed his eyes and counted to ten. A pillow whacked him across the face. Not hard, but enough to rile him further.

"I said leave," she repeated when he remained silent. "I don't want you here."

"Like it or not, you accepted my offer. I'm not leaving," he told her, just so there would be no confusion. He wouldn't leave again until after their baby was born.

"Men." She rolled her eyes. "First you won't come home when I ask you to. Now you won't leave when I order you to. Let's see, maybe I should beg you to stay so that you'll hightail it out the door so fast I'll end up with windburn."

"Maybe." He stood inches from her, meeting her hot gaze head-on, but not once did her glare waver. Instead, her eyes glittered with stubborn challenge. A challenge that compelled him to accept. "Try me and find out."

Only the slight dilation of her pupils gave credence to her surprise at his response, but she quickly masked it behind a fake smile.

"James, would you, please, stay?" she said in a syrupy voice, mocking him with her fluttering lashes. "Please, don't leave." More eyelash flutters. "How's that?"

He'd had enough. He pulled her to him, pressing her round belly and slender body close. Her heat burned through his clothes, her smell inflamed his senses, but it was her eyes that tore him in two. They taunted. Teased. Glowed with the unique light inside this woman who'd bewitched him from the moment they'd met.

"Since when did you get such a smart mouth?"

"I've always had one," she retorted. "You just failed to notice."

"I notice everything about your mouth." His gaze dropped to her slightly parted lips. "Everything."

Her eyes darkened, besieging him with long-denied

need. His gut knotted, his palms itched, his entire body yearned.

He gave in.

Kissed her.

Soft and slow for the first touch of his lips to hers. Tasting the dewy sweet ripeness as if for the first time, cherishing each play of his lips over hers. The slow caresses lasted only seconds before the ache in him took over and he devoured her mouth, demanding that she open, give him access inside.

Inside her mouth, her body, her heart, her soul.

She moaned, squirming, pressing nearer. She twisted her fingers at his nape, pulling him closer, and still they weren't close enough. Not for him. Not for her.

He'd known in his heart, but touching her, holding her confirmed just how miserable he'd been the past couple of months.

Miserable enough that he found the strength to pry his lips from hers.

He ran his palms down her arms and to the small of her back, holding her to him, feeling the full swell of her belly against his hard groin.

Eyes dazed with passion, she blinked up at him. She'd gone from spitting mad to soft, pliant.

"Don't stop." With that, she trailed her tongue over his throat, running it over his carotid pulse and into the indention at his clavicle. "Please, don't stop."

A lightning storm struck everywhere she touched, sending thunderous shock waves throughout his body. Her words shook him just as tumultuously. What was she saying? That she wanted him to kiss her? Or that she wanted him to stay? Make love to her?

He wanted nothing more than to carry her into the bedroom they'd shared during what he now realized had been the best period of his life and do all the things he'd missed doing. To her. With her. But she'd take it wrong, think they could fall right back into old habits, and that wasn't good enough for him.

Not by far.

He caressed her face, wondering how he could have missed just how much she meant to him. Just how far he was willing to go for this woman's well-being.

Because he wasn't doing this just for him or even for their baby. He did it for Melissa. To keep her from working her life away and someday looking around and realizing she had nothing outside her career. No one to love. No one to love her. Because she'd let each relationship wither and die without ever realizing what she was doing.

"James?" she breathed against his neck, her hands splaying across his back. "I want you here, with me. Always."

Always.

Lord, give him strength.

He trapped her wrists and held them, keeping her from rubbing her body against him. "You have to stop, Melissa. This is wrong."

Her dark eyes went round and her body stiff.

He watched all the wrong conclusions form in her mind.

"I forgot," she chided herself, looking embarrassed, lost, disbelieving. "I forgot that you didn't want me anymore."

He ached. His body and his heart. "I do want you, Melissa. I've never stopped wanting you."

She gave him a don't-feed-me-that-garbage look. "I can tell by how you leapt at my offer."

"You didn't mean to make that offer any more than I needed to accept it."

She pulled her wrists free and he let her. Her arms crossed over her chest, and her chin lifted.

"Don't tell me what I meant to do or didn't mean to do. It's become quite apparent that you don't know me nearly as well as you seem to think."

"I know you better than you know yourself."

"Then you'll know that I want you to leave."

"Leaving hasn't solved much in the past. Possibly it's only complicated an already complicated enough situation." He crossed his arms, thinking they probably looked ridiculous facing off against one another. "But at the time it seemed the right thing to do. Now taking care of you is the right thing."

"I don't need you to take care of me."

He remained silent, unyielding.

"Fine. Suit yourself." She gathered up her book and stomped out of the living room in a tantrum he'd have expected from a child but not a woman like Melissa.

Any moment he expected to hear the bedroom door slam, but he only caught the faint sound of her clicking the lock into place. They'd talk later. Melissa's pride was too hurt for them to make any progress tonight.

James went back to his car to grab his overnight bag and the groceries he'd bought. He needed a shower, food, and sleep in that order.

After months of no appetite, why did hers show up full force tonight? Melissa lay on her bed, reading her book, cursing that she was still on the same page she'd been on before James got home an hour ago. Of course, it might be the tantalizing aromas wafting from the kitchen, stimulating her gnawing stomach. James had always been a good cook.

What was he doing? Didn't he know that showing up last night, working at her office today, coming home tonight, cooking in her kitchen now, that all those things confused her?

Maybe she was over-analyzing his motives.

He'd told her their baby's well-being drove his actions.

Could it be that simple? That once the baby was born he'd step out of her life except for the awkward moments of dropping off their child or picking him up?

When he'd held her, kissed her, he hadn't felt like a man who had no feelings for her, though. Quite the opposite. The attraction still existed between them. Strong, powerful, demanding.

An attraction that she hadn't had the strength to deny.

Hadn't wanted to deny.

One touch of his lips and she'd been ready to drag him back into her bed.

He'd wanted her. No words could convince her otherwise. She had felt the evidence of his desire. So why had he pushed her away?

* * *

James munched on a carrot and surveyed the meal he'd thrown together. Baked chicken breasts over a bed of wild rice, green beans, fresh carrot sticks that she must have purchased sometime during the past week, bread rolls because, quite frankly, she needed the carbs, and apple sauce for desert.

He poured two glasses of milk and set them on the table.

Now the question was whether or not Melissa was going to stay in her room pouting all night.

Nursing her wounds might be more accurate.

Because he'd hurt her. Not intentionally, but he wouldn't lie to her. He didn't want their old life back. Not ever.

Not that he didn't want Melissa, but he wanted commitment. Mental, physical, emotional, spiritual, he wanted it all.

And, damn it, tonight, when she'd looked at him, he'd have sworn Melissa wanted the same thing.

Definitely, she wanted him physically.

His stomach flip-flopped at the memory of her body pressed against his, of her sweet plea not to stop. How he'd found the strength, he didn't know. Even now he hungered to burst into her bedroom, push her back on her bed, and have his way with her body, starting at her mouth and working his way down, kissing every inch of her delectable flesh, discovering firsthand the changes to her blossoming body.

If he made love to her, he'd be a slave to the power she held over him. He'd fall victim to the need to have her again and again. And he'd never be able to leave after the baby came. He wondered how he'd manage that anyway.

He had to tell her about Cailee. Soon. But not yet. He couldn't bear it if he looked in her eyes and saw the disgust he felt toward himself for his mistakes.

Sighing, he knocked on her bedroom door. "Melissa? Dinner's ready."

No answer. Big surprise.

"You need to eat. For the baby."

He heard movement, then the door opened and, without looking at him, she marched past.

James watched her head toward the kitchen in an almost six-months pregnant waddle. At least she planned to eat.

He'd keep the conversation light, establish peace between them. For the next few months his whole world would revolve around making Melissa's life easier.

James listened to Caren Little, a hefty sixty-year-old who appeared much older, go on and on about her husband's bunions, her daughters ignoring her, her neighbor's penchant for gossiping, her second cousin Bertha's cheating husband, and how the pharmaceutical companies were ripping off the poor. Surreptitiously, he glanced at his watch.

How long could she drone on without getting to the point of why she was at the clinic?

"So, what exactly is it that I can do for you today?" he finally asked.

She gave him a startled look. "Nothing, child."

Child? He'd choose to ignore that, but *nothing*?

"Mrs Little, you understand that there are other patients waiting to see me? That my time is valuable, and if there's nothing I can do for you, you've taken up time I could have spent with another patient." He pinned her with a direct stare. "Why are you here?"

The woman's wrinkled face drew into a frown and her chubby arms crossed. Unwaveringly, she met his gaze with her arcus-rimmed pupils. He mentally made a note to check her cholesterol levels as fatty deposits in the eye caused the light ring to form.

"To see Dr Melissa, of course." Her expression said she thought he was the one missing a few marbles.

This was Melissa's practice, a practice she loved, so he remained diplomatic, pleasant even as he smiled at the woman. "She's not here this afternoon."

Melissa had gone to see Dr McGowan that afternoon. He'd wanted to go with her, but that meant closing the office, and she wouldn't hear of it. They'd worked out a compromise and he went every other visit. That way he could at least keep current on what was going on with the baby.

The woman gave him a worried look. "But she will be back tomorrow, right? I really need to see her. It's a matter of life and death."

A matter of life and death? That sounded more up his alley. Pleased that they were finally getting somewhere, James took the woman's hand in his and gave her a reassuring smile.

"Mrs Little, if it's that urgent, I can take care of you today and then you won't need to see Dr Conner tomorrow."

The woman's drawn-on-with-a-black-pencil brows V'd. "But you don't even know what's wrong with me."

Exactly. "Then perhaps you will enlighten me so we can take care of this life-and-death matter."

She pulled her hands free and tightened her arms across her chest in a protective gesture. "But you're not Dr Melissa."

"No." His patience wore thin. "But I am a trained medical doctor and am more than qualified to take care of any medical issue you have. Particularly life-or-death ones."

She didn't look impressed. Neither did she budge an inch from her stance, just gave him a smug look. "Qualified doesn't mean you can do squat for my problem."

"True enough." He took a deep breath. "But if you tell me what ails you, we can determine if I can or if you need an appointment with Dr Conner tomorrow."

The woman's gaze dropped to her abundant lap, as did her hands. She wrung her arthritic fingers. "I can't sleep at night," she admitted.

Finally. "Insomnia is a common problem. I'll give you a handout on some lifestyle tips to make sure you aren't causing the insomnia through diet or behavior." He scribbled some remarks in her chart. "I'll also write you a prescription."

That drawn-on brow so in contrast to her shock of white hair lifted. "Ain't no sleeping pill going to help me sleep."

"How would you know that?" He'd reviewed Mrs Little's chart and hadn't seen any documentation of medication trials. The woman rarely came in other than for a refill on her heart medicines and the occasional upper respiratory infection.

She tossed another look that said he wasn't right. "Because you didn't ask why I ain't sleeping."

James had to give credit where credit was due. She had a point. He hadn't asked. He'd been in too big a hurry to move on to the next patient so he could finish his day and check on Melissa. He wanted to know what Dr McGowan had told her, how the baby was progressing, though mainly he just wanted to see Melissa.

"Why can't you sleep, Mrs Little?" he asked, hoping he didn't sound patronizing. He had no doubt the older woman would call him on it if he did.

"'Cos Mr Little won't let me."

James suspected he was the one wearing that missing-a-few-marbles look now. "He snores?" he guessed.

The woman frowned. "All his life, but what does that have to do with my not sleeping?"

James sat the chart down on the counter. "Mrs Little, could you, please, just tell me what Mr Little is doing that's keeping you from sleeping?"

"Not if you're going to take that tone of voice, young man." Her arms crossed and she locked up as tight as Fort Knox.

James bit back his natural inclination and instead coated his words with sugar. "I'm sorry, Mrs Little. I'm here to help and really do want to help you get some sleep. If you can just tell me what the problem is, perhaps we can arrange for you to get a good night's rest."

She gave him a doubtful look, but shrugged. "It's that prescription stuff Dr Melissa gave my husband."

James felt as lost as before they'd started the conversation. "What prescription would that be?"

"That blue pill," she said with total loathing.

"Blue pill?"

"You know." She gave him a look that said he definitely should know what she was talking about. "That Viagra stuff that makes men not let their wives sleep. Now, what are you going to do to help me get a decent night's sleep?"

Melissa waddled like a bloated penguin. Her feet hurt. Her face looked puffy. Her bladder was the size of a pea. And her lower back hurt twenty-four hours a day.

But she wore a smile most of the time.

Because of the man who sat with her feet in his lap. While reading an article in *Emergency Medicine*, he absently massaged her arches.

They'd fallen into a routine and, if only he'd loved her, she'd be in heaven.

Because she did want James's love.

If there had ever been any doubt in her mind, there no longer was. He completed her, made her feel capable of conquering the world. Those weeks without him had proved that life wasn't much without him to share it.

Sure, she loved her practice, but her career made for a lonely bed partner.

And she did crawl into bed alone every night.

Not once had James set foot into their room. Would she ever stop thinking of it as "their" room?

His fingers trailed lightly over her toes and she met his gaze, catching him watching her. A glimpse of lust dissipated almost immediately, making her wonder if she'd imagined it.

"You OK?" he asked, when she continued looking at him.

How could she not be? Every moment he was there, touching her, she wanted to store it all in her memory. Store it for the empty nights she'd have after he moved to Nashville for good.

She caressed her stomach. "The baby's just wiggling a lot tonight." True enough. Based on what an energy ball their son was in utero, she suspected he'd give his parents a run for their money.

James's gaze dropped to her belly. His eyes widened when the mound of flesh shifted beneath her cotton maternity top.

He dropped his magazine onto the coffee table and scooted closer. "May I?"

He wanted to touch her belly? Other than her feet and calves, he didn't touch her, not since the night he'd moved home. Sometimes she thought he purposely avoided touching her, despite the fact that she yearned for his touch.

Nodding, she took his hand and guided it to where it was sure to receive a quick jab. Mere seconds passed before her belly bumped against James's hand.

"Amazing." He placed his other hand against her belly and cradled her between his palms. The fabric from her shirt bunched and he tugged at it, trying to smooth it.

Melissa made a quick decision. Her heart thumping and feeling almost shy, she placed her hand over his and guided the fabric upward, revealing the pale, stretched flesh.

James's gaze followed her movements, but he didn't comment, just slid his hands over her bare belly, cupping the fullness as if it were the most precious thing he'd ever touched.

It likely was, she realized.

True to his nature, the baby showed off under his father's attention. Kicking and jabbing at Melissa's insides with the fervor of a manic on a caffeine high. Perhaps the rush of adrenaline and hormones surging through his mother spurred the little fellow on.

James touched her. Really touched her.

How long they sat like that she wasn't sure. Only that when their gazes met, such tenderness glowed from his blue eyes that her throat knotted and her chest constricted into a tight band around her lungs.

She loved him. With all her heart. All her soul. All of who she was.

And he'd loved her, too. Although he may not have realized it, she knew he had.

Only she'd let his love slip through her fingers without ever knowing what a precious gift she'd had.

James jerked his hands away from her belly, as if he'd looked into her eyes and been scalded by her thoughts.

His gaze took on a faraway look. "I had a sister."

A sister? She'd never heard him mention a sister. She stared at him, saw the sheen of sweat on his brow, the pallor to his skin, the lost depths to his eyes.

And she knew what he was going to say even before he continued and her heart shattered into a million pieces at the pain inside him.

* * *

"Cailee was a surprise to my parents. They were in their early forties. I had turned seventeen a few months before she was born and was checking into colleges. I wanted to be a computer programmer." At her surprised look, he gave an ironic nod. "My mom suffered from postnatal depression after Cailee's birth and my dad decided taking her out for the evening might lift her spirits. I was to watch Cailee and wasn't happy about it. I'd had plans to go hang out with some buddies."

Memories assailed him and he could almost hear Tyler and Ryan's voices as they kidded him on playing nanny. "Instead, they came to the house. Cailee was sleeping and we played video games."

He stopped, collecting his thoughts, his courage so he could push on. Keeping his gaze averted for fear of what he'd see, he began again.

"After they left, I checked on her. I thought she was just sleeping." He relived the panicked horror that had drenched him as he'd realized Cailee's little chest hadn't been rising and falling with the sweet baby sounds of slumber. "I was wrong."

"Was it SIDS?" Emotions choked her words. Tears flooded her eyes and fell onto her cheeks.

James didn't answer her question, just continued. "I tried to revive her, but I didn't know what to do. My efforts were useless. I couldn't bring her back." His voice broke and he stopped, unable to go on without losing the calm control he desperately clung to.

"Oh, James, how tragic. I'm so sorry."

"It was SIDS, apparently. At the time I'd never even heard of it. But I know the tragedy was because of my negligence. If I'd checked, kept my eye on her like I was supposed to, she wouldn't have died."

"You were only a child yourself," she defended him. "You can't watch over a sleeping baby every second of every minute. It really wasn't your fault, James. Surely your parents didn't blame you."

"No," he admitted. His parents had never once voiced what he knew in his heart. It had been his fault. "They were too busy blaming each other to ever blame me. They divorced less than six months after Cailee's death."

"You lost your whole family that summer," she said, pity softening her words. "That's why you didn't want children? Because of what happened with Cailee?"

James wanted her pity even less than he wanted her disgust. Why had he told her? Because feeling the baby move within her womb had made it so much more real that he was going to be a father. And he should be scared, keeping himself aloof. Instead, excitement filled him. He wanted this baby.

And that realization did scare him.

"Now you know." He gathered his magazine, stood, and turned away from her. "It's been a long day." He faked a yawn. "I'm calling it a night."

"James, wait." She reached for his hand, squeezed it. "Let's talk about this."

"No, I've said all I'm saying on the matter. You wanted to know my reasons." He pulled free from her grasp and headed out of the room. He'd said all he had to say and just wanted to escape her piteous eyes. "Now you do, and it changes nothing."

CHAPTER TEN

MELISSA swore her belly was going to burst if she gained another ounce. Already breathing had become a major ordeal and not much was worth the effort of moving. Thirty-nine weeks pregnant, feet swollen, hands swollen, belly definitely swollen, and backache that increased each day. It took all her willpower to keep going.

But she did keep going.

Like today. Barely ten in the morning and already she'd seen a half dozen patients. She rubbed her lower back, wishing the pain would ease, knowing from her experience over the past week that it wouldn't.

"The next room is Jamie Moss," Debbie said, taking it on herself to rub Melissa's tight belly.

Everyone seemed to think it their right to touch her stomach, like she was some type of pregnant Buddha to rub for fortune or entertainment. Melissa smiled to herself. No one seemed able to resist the lure of the well-rounded belly.

"How's Junior doing?" Debbie handed Jamie's chart to Melissa.

"Kicking for all he's worth." She forced a smile,

taking the chart. Although she still didn't know for certain, she'd taken to calling the baby "he". James hadn't corrected her, neither had he batted an eyelash when she bought blue item after blue item.

"What about Mom?"

"She's holding up." Holding up, but living inside a glasshouse she expected to shatter around her at a moment's notice.

"James called to check on you." Debbie's gaze bore into her, seeing through the façade Melissa wore.

Not for one minute did Melissa think she was fooling her friend.

"He's convinced he should have canceled out this semester." Her friend looked at her thoughtfully. "He seems so besotted with you. How are things at home?"

In some ways home was wonderful. She spent lots of time each evening with James. Occasionally they made house calls together. Occasionally, when he knew the patient, he went alone. But more and more she was routing her patients through the Dekalb emergency room or, if possible, having them wait until the following day before she saw them in the office. Plus, her patients seemed to sense that with her pregnancy she had to cut back and fewer infringed on her evening hours.

But James held back. Emotionally and physically. He refused to discuss Cailee and when she tried, he'd immediately shut her out.

Melissa shrugged in response to Debbie's question. "He's the perfect father-to-be, making sure I eat right, keep my feet propped up, rubbing my back." She wished his magic hands were rubbing right now, because Junior was using her spine for a punching bag, her ribs for a soccer ball. Punch. Kick. Kick.

"I meant between the two of you."

"Nothing different." Wasn't that what he'd said after telling her about Cailee? That nothing had changed? Melissa stretched her spine, hoping to ease the pressure and her heartache. "He plans to leave after the baby is born."

Debbie's eyes narrowed. "Do you think he'll really go?"

Yeah, she thought he would leave. Just last week a realtor had called about a house he'd looked at. In Nashville. Which she refused to think about now. She'd deal with that later, after the baby came. But she worried about how James would handle fatherhood. Would he see Cailee every time he looked at their baby? How could she help him if he refused to talk to her?

He was right. Nothing had changed. They were still holding back from each other.

She swallowed back the thoughts that haunted her night after night. Thoughts that ranged from James walking away from her and the baby to him becoming so besotted with their child that he fought for full custody.

"I should see Jamie now."

Debbie nodded, letting Melissa change the subject.

"Hi, Jamie," Melissa said, entering the exam room. "How are you feeling today?"

Debbie had written "Talk" in the chart so Jamie couldn't have told her why she'd come in.

Jamie had lost weight. Her eyebrows had fallen out months ago, and although she'd finished her chemo, they hadn't started growing back yet. As with each time Melissa had seen her, Jamie's eyes were red and puffy as if she spent most of her time crying.

"I'm not sure where to start." Jamie stared at her hands.

"Are the girls OK?" Melissa prompted, when Jamie visibly struggled to find words.

"Things aren't good at home."

"Financially?"

"Money is a problem, but it always has been." Jamie put her hands under her jeans-clad legs. "After everything you've done for me, I don't know how to say this."

Melissa's heart filled with dread. Something bad was going on.

"I'm through."

Uh-oh. "Through?"

"I'm tired." Jamie's eyes beseeched Melissa to understand. "Too tired. I can't fight this anymore."

"The girls—"

"Wish I was dead." Tears streamed down Jamie's face. "And so do I."

"Oh, Jamie. We've discussed this in the past. You know they don't mean it. You've come so far." Jamie had made it through her chemotherapy, through her mastectomy, and was now having her radiation treatments. "You're beating the cancer, Jamie. Dr Arnold told me so."

Jamie's face pinched at the mention of the surgeon's name.

"I lost a long time ago, long before Roger died. Maybe from the moment I married him." The woman swiped at her tears. "I've tried to do what's right, be there for my girls, but they'd be better off without me."

"That isn't true. Cindy and Amanda need you. So much."

"You're wrong. Cindy is having trouble in school. She's run away from home twice in the past month. Amanda cries herself to sleep every night, asking for Roger. I'm at my wits' end."

"The school counselor hasn't helped?"

Jamie's gaze dropped. "She says it's my fault the girls haven't dealt with Roger's death."

"She said what?" Apparently the only counselor available was doing more harm than good. Melissa would be placing a call to the school counselor to find out what was going on.

"It doesn't matter." Jamie lifted her shoulders. "I just wanted you to know I appreciate everything you've done."

"Jamie." Melissa made eye contact and gave voice to what she'd feared from the moment Jamie had made her admission, "You're scaring me. You sound suicidal."

Jamie looked down, fiddled with her bitten-to-the-quick fingernails.

"Are you thinking of killing yourself, Jamie?" Melissa held her breath, waiting for an answer she didn't want to hear.

"I want to die."

"How?" *Please, don't have a plan.*

"I just want to go to sleep and not wake up."

"Do you have a plan, Jamie? A way to make yourself go to sleep and not wake up?"

She hesitated long enough that warning bells went off in Melissa's head. "I've thought about taking more of my insulin than I should. I'd just go into a coma and not wake up again."

She had a plan on how to kill herself.

"Jamie, I think you're telling me this because you don't want to die, but are scared by your feelings." Melissa took her hand. "I want to help you, but I'm not able to provide the care you need. I'm going to send you to get special help."

"No." Jamie shook her head. "I can't go anywhere. What would I do with the girls?"

"What would happen to them if you weren't here, Jamie? If you died, where would they go? Do you think your sister could handle another two? Even if she tried, it would be difficult."

Jamie's eyes closed.

"You need help that I'm not qualified to give. I'm going to call your sister, ask her to take the girls for a few days."

"She won't."

Something more was going on. "Why not?"

"She's not speaking to me."

Which might have been the straw that had broken the camel's back.

"Did you argue?" she asked gently.

Jamie nodded.

"What happened?"

Jamie shook her head. "I don't want to talk about it."

"If this is what's made you want to die, you need to talk about it."

"It's not."

Melissa didn't believe her. Jamie had remained so strong through it all, an ideal patient, according to Dr

Arnold. Dr Arnold had taken a special interest in Jamie. Even when Melissa and he talked about other patients, Jamie's name always came into the conversation. Always. And the interest sounded more and more personal rather than professional.

Jamie had a lot to live for. Dr Arnold was a good man.

Melissa weighed her options. She could have Jamie committed if she believed she intended to hurt herself. She looked at the blond woman, shoulders slumped, eyes dejected.

Did she think Jamie would really hurt herself? That was the million-dollar question.

Jamie was crying out for help and had no one to turn to except her. She wouldn't risk being wrong.

"I'm going to call the crisis hotline. A counselor will come to the office to talk with you. I think they'll advise you to go to the hospital for a while."

Jamie's eyes widened in protest.

"If your sister can't watch the girls, I'll look after them."

Jamie's gaze dropped to Melissa's belly, reminding her that her timing might be off for making such a grand gesture.

"I'm not due for another week. It'll be fine." Somehow it would be. She would see to it.

Jamie shook her head. "I can't ask you to do that."

"Isn't that the wonderful thing about friends?" Melissa squeezed her hand. "You didn't have to ask. I offered."

Lunchtime came, but talking with the crisis counselor put Melissa behind and she hadn't finished with her morning patients. Still, she stopped for a yogurt and an apple. She'd made James a promise and would do her best to live up to that promise.

For the past two weeks he'd refused to let her work full time. She hadn't wanted to give in, but had, for James. He'd lived up to his end of the bargain. Her practice flourished, and she was honest enough to admit that she would have had to cut back even if James hadn't forced the issue. His help kept things moving normally, better than normal. He saw patients with her on Mondays, Wednesdays, and Fridays, lightening her workload tremendously. And for the past month he'd come home early on Tuesdays and Thursdays, insisting she get some rest.

Today, she wouldn't argue. Her back throbbed.

Fortunately, Jamie's worried sister agreed to take the girls, but would need them picked up from school. Cindy had to stay for detention each afternoon due to not doing her homework.

"How's your day been?" James asked, arriving at the clinic, slipping off his coat and doing the obligatory belly rub.

Even knowing that he touched the baby rather than her, Melissa's pulse quickened. When the baby gave a hearty push against his hand, James smiled. Heat filled Melissa at the tenderness in his blue eyes. He would be OK. Together they would deal with his past, with Cailee's death.

"OK for the most part." She started to tell him about Jamie, but Debbie knocked on the office door.

"Sorry to interrupt, but Ben Brown is in the procedure room. He sliced his hand open while cutting wood. He's bleeding pretty badly."

"I'll be right there," James told the nurse, then smiled at Melissa. "I'll take care of Ben. Go home. You look tired."

"It has been a long day," she admitted, wishing they'd had time to talk about Jamie. In the past they'd rarely talked about patients. These days they shared insights and smiles over the day's events. They would talk tonight.

The weather took a turn for the worse and a few snowflakes fell from the gray sky. Melissa left her car running and, bundled up in her oversized coat, waddled into the school.

When Amanda saw her, heard why Melissa was there, she started crying. "She's dead, isn't she? I wished her dead, and now she is. Just like my daddy."

Startled by Amanda's unexpected reaction, Melissa wrapped her arms around the little girl, held her sobbing body, offering words of comfort.

Obviously thinking similarly to her sister, Cindy crouched on the floor, hugged her knees to her chest, and curled into a ball. Eyes closed, she rocked back and forth.

Not knowing if she'd be able to get up, Melissa lowered herself to the floor, pulling Amanda and Cindy to her. The three of them embraced, crying together for what seemed like hours. Melissa cried for Jamie, for the girls, for what should have been between her and James.

Some time later, tears all dried, Amanda eyed Melissa's dilemma. "We need a bulldozer."

"I think you mean a crane." Melissa smiled.

The girls each took a hand and between them and the

teacher who'd stood by, nervously watching them huddle on the school floor, Melissa managed to get to her feet.

But not without a new stab of pain across her back. A sharp one that stole her breath. Fortunately, it lasted only seconds, but she didn't need James to know she'd overdone it.

The girls looked so forlorn when she told them where she planned to take them that she didn't have it in her to just drop them off and leave. Instead, she drove to Dekalb, bought meals from a fast-food chain and explained what she could of what Jamie wanted her daughters to know about her depression.

They listened to Melissa's explanations with an understanding in their eyes that belied their ages. Then again, they'd lived through hell the past year.

Although Jamie would still face a lot of issues when she came home, they would be more supportive. Jamie would have the girls and Dr Arnold, who Melissa had contacted. Admitting that he had feelings for Jamie, he planned to drive to Nashville.

Despite the chilly, snowy weather, Amanda wanted an ice-cream cone. Melissa gave Cindy the money to purchase one and watched the girls go hand in hand to pay for it.

Her phone rang.

She glanced at the displayed number and her heart tripped. "Hello, James."

"Where are you? I finished early and expected to find you asleep."

"I'm in Dekalb."

Silence. "Everything OK?"

"Fine." Except that her back was killing her and Jamie had been hospitalized for suicidal ideations and she'd lost the best thing that had ever happened to her—him.

"Debbie told me about Jamie Moss." Had he read her mind? "I knew you'd be upset. That's why I hurried home."

Home. These past few weeks with him, it had felt like home. But James would leave and home would no longer be home. Home was where the heart was and hers lay with James.

Her gaze fell on the two young girls watching her curiously. All they'd faced hit her again with full force. Life was so short, so precious.

In that moment she knew that she could deal with the fallout of James leaving, but not idly or with acceptance. He may think he was going back to Nashville after their baby was born, but she'd pack the baby's things and her own and follow him. Now that she knew why he kept the world at bay, she'd find a way around those protective walls and heal his heart.

He'd loved her once and she'd do whatever it took to nurture and restore those feelings.

"Melissa?" James said, reminding her that he was on the phone.

"I'll be home in about an hour." She hoped he didn't catch the break in her voice. Why had she gone weepy-eyed? "I've got to take the girls to Jamie's sister."

He hesitated, as if he suspected more was going on. Perhaps he thought her emotional state was because of Jamie. Just wait until she told him the truth.

"Be careful," he warned. "The roads are dangerously slippery."

The roads were treacherous. Snow had turned to sleet and sheets of ice pelted her car. The drive took twice as long as it should have. She feared losing control on the icy road.

By the time she pulled into her garage, the ache in her back had increased to the point where it was all she could do not to cry out with pain. She leaned forward, resting her head on the steering wheel. Rubbing her hands over her lower back, she tried to figure out how to tell James all the things in her heart.

Her car door opened and James touched her shoulder. "You OK?"

She looked up, startled. He must have rushed out the second he'd heard the garage door. What did that mean?

"Not really," she admitted, searching his eyes for a clue about his feelings. He cared, but did he love her? Another spasm shot pain down her legs. "My back is killing me."

"I knew something was up. You didn't sound yourself." His gaze traveled over her in concern. "Any contractions?"

"My belly's been tight, but no contractions."

"The baby's movements are normal?"

"His feet have played contact sport with my ribs all day." Even now she wanted to take her hands and push downward near her ribs in the hope of repositioning the baby. Not that she could. There wasn't room. "Help me?"

He took her hand, easing her out of the vehicle and into the house. He held her arm, slowly lowering her into an oversized chair. When she leaned back, he removed her shoes and propped her feet on a footstool.

He treated her like she was a helpless child, but between her thoughts and the all too real pain in her back, she didn't care.

"Better?" He rubbed the arches of her feet.

"Much." Not really, but after a few minutes of relaxation, getting over that horrible drive, the pain would ease. Besides, the tender, concerned look in James's eyes was enough to make her feel better regardless of her back.

She wanted to be with him. To sleep in his arms and to wake up to the feel, smell, and sight of him next to her.

And she had to tell him. Now.

"I wish I'd married you when I had the chance."

CHAPTER ELEVEN

JAMES'S fingers paused from working their magic on her aching feet.

When the silence stretched, she glanced at where he knelt on the floor. His face masked, he watched her with eyes gone midnight blue.

His thumbs pressed into the balls of her feet and rotated outwards. Although not painful, his touch changed, became strained, tense.

"We could remedy that."

Her heart thudded to a halt. Was he saying what she thought he was saying? "You'd marry me?"

His grip on her foot tightened almost imperceptibly. "It would solve custody issues."

Custody issues. For the breadth of a heartbeat, she'd thought he wanted her. How could she have forgotten the baby? The baby's health and well-being were his number one priorities.

She wanted James in her life, but not at the expense of his happiness.

"What about Nashville?"

He frowned. "What about it?"

She leaned forward, meaning to place her hand over his and tell him she'd go anywhere in the world, just so long as she was with him, but her belly got in the way and a sharp pain slashed across her low back. A strangled cry tore from her lips.

Gripping the armrests with clammy palms, she breathed deeply. The pain would ease. She shut her eyes and concentrated on remaining calm, focusing on her breathing. In. Out.

Damp heat washed over her body and another stabbing pain hit. Had her body just split in two?

This pain was unlike any she'd ever had. Intense. Bone-breaking. Flesh-wrenching.

She opened her eyes, met James's look of total disbelief. Laughter gurgled from her lips.

Laughter full of fear and on the verge of hysteria.

James stared at Melissa. Moisture beaded along her forehead. Her hands gripped the edge of the chair tightly. Her knuckles blanched a ghostly white and dug deeply into the knobby fabric.

"Melissa?"

Her wild-eyed gaze met his briefly before her eyes closed in a painful grimace.

"You're having contractions, aren't you?"

"My back hurts. Bad," Melissa squeaked, placing her hand over her tight belly. "Yeah, I think I'm having contractions."

His heart performed a contraction of its own, an intense one that caused every muscle in his body to compress sharply at what he knew was taking place.

Air was trapped in his lungs. He was a doctor, had seen babies delivered before, had even delivered during a rotation. But this was Melissa. In labor with his baby. Right this minute.

Cailee's face swam before his eyes. Memories of walking to her crib, finding her lifeless body, his mother's heartache, his father's bouts of depression, the fights that had followed Cailee's funeral, the guilt that he'd not been able to save her—all these things and more prostrated him.

"James?" she said, when he remained frozen.

Snapping out of his trance, he met her gaze. "We'll call Dr McGowan, have him meet us at the hospital. It'll be all right," he offered, hoping to ease the tension flowing from her body, but more than anything to keep her from seeing the fear that coursed through his body.

"And you know this, how?" Melissa growled, not sounding at all like herself. "It isn't your body being ripped in two."

Wanna bet? But he didn't say the words out loud. She didn't look in the mood to debate the similarity of sensations they were experiencing.

"How far apart are your contractions?" James asked, kicking into doctor mode. "When did they start? Is the pain bad?"

"I don't know, I'm not sure, and *yes*," she responded.

She looked scared. He had to do something. Somehow make this easier for her. He pried her hands from their death hold on the armrests and clasped them.

"Everything is going to be fine. Dr McGowan is an excellent obstetrician. The best."

He'd meant his words to comfort her. Instead, her fingers bit into his. Her eyes widened with surprise, and then she glanced down in horror at the growing stain on her pants.

"James," she gasped. "My waters have broken."

No turning back now. They were going to be parents. Soon.

He looked at her, wishing he could still the tremble in the abused lip locked between her teeth.

"I'm going to get you a towel, call Dr McGowan, and then get your medical bag. While I'm doing that, I want you to time your contractions."

"Quit talking slow to me. I'm having a baby, not losing my mind." She winced, her body tightening. "I am losing my mind. James!" His name came out as a cry. A cry full of pain and longing. Full of need.

For him to slay her dragons.

"Melissa, if that's another contraction, they're really close." He mentally calculated how much time had passed, his heart picking up rhythm with the realization that she was close to giving birth. Too close. "I should check you."

She scowled. "I don't think so."

"I'm a doctor."

"Not my doctor."

"Fine." Stubborn woman. He hurried to the bathroom and grabbed a stack of fluffy navy towels to place between her legs to soak up the leaking amniotic fluid.

He tossed the towels onto the footstool.

"I'm calling Dr McGowan." Keeping his eyes on Melissa, James hit the programmed-in number on his cell phone and informed the obstetrician what was going on.

"How far dilated is she?" Dr McGowan asked.

"I don't know." James watched Melissa's face distort in misery. Sweat trickled down her brow. He glanced at his watch. "Her contractions are coming a minute apart."

"A minute apart?" the obstetrician exclaimed. "How long has she been in labor?"

"Her waters broke about five minutes ago, but her back's been hurting all day."

"She doesn't have time to get to Nashville. Check her cervix and you make the call, but I think you should call an ambulance to take her to Dekalb."

Watching Melissa's hands fist into tight bundles, James feared Dr McGowan might be right.

"Check her and let me know."

He snapped his cell phone shut. "I've got to check you."

"No." Her denial came out as a breathy moan.

He hated seeing her in pain, wished he could ease her suffering. Even more, he'd hate to put her in the car and head to Nashville an hour away and have her deliver somewhere along the icy drive.

"It's nothing I haven't seen before," he reminded her.

She shot him a look.

Maybe not the smoothest line he'd ever used.

"With your contractions so close, Dr McGowan wants to know how dilated you are. He thinks I need to call an ambulance to take you to Dekalb."

Cheeks flushed, she closed her eyes. "Fine, but it's not like I have a spare set of stirrups just lying around to hike my legs up in."

"This will be fine." He eyed the chair and stool. "I'm going to get a flashlight and some gloves."

James gathered what he'd need to check Melissa and scrubbed his hands and forearms. Her smothered cry of pain warned that she was having another contraction. From the sounds she was making he'd guess her pain was intensifying.

Helplessness seized him. A helplessness he'd sworn he'd never feel again after Cailee's death. What if the baby was breech? Melissa's life would be in danger, would be in his hands. He swallowed the lump forming in his throat. What had Kristen called Melissa? His heart's desire. She was, and so much more.

And he was responsible for her life and their baby's life. He didn't want to do it, but there was no choice.

"I'm coming," he called, wanting her to know she wasn't alone, that he'd stay by her side. Forever, if that's what she wanted.

"I need to push." She moaned, making him think he couldn't possibly have heard right. "James, I need to push."

"Push?" He rushed into the living room and dropped his supplies in a heap next to her chair. "You can't push."

"Don't tell me what I can and can't do," she growled, very un-Melissa-like. "My body says push."

He helped her to her feet, winced at her whimper. With his assistance, she removed her wet maternity pants and underwear. Despite the urgency of the moment, he paused, staring at her rounded belly. Her creamy skin stretched tight over what could easily have been a lumpy basketball.

His knees threatened to buckle at the sheer beauty of her carrying his child. Would he be wrong if he dropped to the floor and praised her over and over for the precious gift she carried? A gift he couldn't believe he'd once thought he wanted to live without experiencing because of a fear of Cailee's memory, of a fear of love, of a fear of failure.

Just as he'd once thought he could live without Melissa. Now he knew better. Not loving would be the biggest failure of his life. He'd take Melissa on any terms she'd have him. He'd find a way to help keep her grounded, focused on him and their child. Because these past few months, watching her, seeing her lovingly touch her belly, excitedly prepare the nursery, he knew she was going to be a good mother. To place their child's needs above her own. Above those of her patients.

Her goodness and ability would balance out any fears on his part. He could live with coming in somewhere down the line. Just so long as he was still in the line.

She'd said she wished she'd married him when she'd had the chance.

He wished he'd gotten down on his knees and begged her to be his wife, to share his life, for them to bring their baby into the world as a family, as one.

For that matter, he should have proposed the day they'd made love for the first time. He'd known even then that she completed him.

He thought of the diamond ring in the spare bedroom. The engagement ring he'd bought with all the excitement of a man in love. Because he had been. Was.

Why had he held back? For fear of hurting? *Stupid.* From the moment they'd met, he should have told her every day how he felt. Had he been open with her, perhaps they never would have grown apart. He should have told her about Cailee and his parents, about his fears of losing a child and how it had led to his foolish decision to not be a parent.

Not caring if she thought him a fool, he cupped her stomach, stroked his palms over the roundness, felt the outline of their baby.

Her cheeks pink, she seemed to want to cover herself, but knew there was no way to hide her burgeoning beauty.

And just so there was no mistake that he touched her as a man in awe rather than as a doctor, he sank to his knees and kissed her stomach.

Beneath his touch, the skin on her belly drew tight, the muscles constricting. She grabbed his shoulder and squeezed, her nails digging through his shirt.

She panted, squeezing harder and harder.

"I really need to push, James. It feels like he's coming out." Her pitch grew higher. "Right now."

"Let me check you."

Helping her back into the chair, he draped the blanket he'd brought over her waist, knowing she wanted some semblance of privacy.

"For the record," she said, her contraction subsiding, "I don't like this and am only agreeing because I swear he feels like he's right there."

"You don't have to like it. It's only a medical check. The same as if Dr McGowan was checking."

"Yeah, right," she said from between gritted teeth.

James spread her thighs and nearly had a heart attack at what he saw. At least, his heart sure felt like it had stopped.

Melissa felt the need to push because the baby's head had crowned. She was fully dilated and didn't have time to go to Dekalb, much less Vanderbilt.

"What's wrong?" She craned her neck, trying to get a better look at his face. "James?"

"There's no time."

When he didn't move, she asked, "You're going to call the ambulance?"

"They won't make it in time for the delivery."

"How do you know?"

"Because I can see you're fully dilated. A few big pushes and we'll be welcoming our child into the world."

"Oh," Melissa mouthed, fear in her eyes. Another contraction hit. Involuntarily, her back arched.

Without moving away, he dialed for an ambulance.

"Tell me I can push," she begged, the moment he'd hung up from the dispatcher who'd wanted him to stay on the line, but he hadn't wanted the distraction. There was nothing she could tell him that he didn't already know. Unlike with Cailee, he knew what to do.

"Because I need to push," she continued.

Thanking God for his medical training, James quickly checked the baby's position. Face down. Not breech, which he'd known from when he'd cradled her belly. Perfect.

He sent up a silent prayer of gratitude.

"Push, but remember to use your contraction to your advantage. Push in conjunction with your body's efforts."

"My back is breaking." Her eyes were feral, begging his for reassurance, for relief.

"I know, babe," he soothed, "but you've got to work

with your contraction. Let's wait till this one passes, and we'll work together on the next one."

She panted through the contraction, her fingers digging into the chair.

Seconds strung out, passing in slow motion. Finally the contraction ended and Melissa had a quick breather. Her hair was wet around her face, her skin glistened, and her knuckles remained embedded in the chair arms.

His heart swelled with love, with joy, with the pain she was enduring, with fear at what her body was going through, and that he would be facing his worst fear soon. But there was no time to dwell on any of that. Her abdomen tightened and her back arched. Another contraction was starting.

"Push as hard as you can, and we'll have our baby."

CHAPTER TWELVE

As HARD as she could? Melissa glared at James. Was he kidding?

Right now it was all she could do to breathe, much less push. But the pressure did make her want to push. To relieve her body of the enormous heaviness weighing on her pelvis.

How had women done this for centuries?

Women gave birth and then went right back out to the fields to pick cotton? Lies. All lies. Had to be.

Drugs. She needed drugs. Lots of them. Anything to ease the torture she was suffering.

Bits and pieces of her maternity rotations came back to her. Pieces that told her how to regulate her breathing, how to naturally ease the pressure in her body.

It was time for their baby to enter the world, and she had to find the strength to help him. To push so mightily he couldn't resist the lure of the world any longer.

She panted. Focused. Panted.

"Push, sweetheart," James encouraged from between her legs. "You can do it. I can see the top of the baby's head."

He could?

More pain and pressure tore at her body. A pain so intense she'd swear her hips were being plucked apart.

"James," she cried, bearing down as hard as she could.

"That's it, babe. *Push*."

Melissa pushed, holding her breath and bearing down, hard. Harder. Harder still.

"Breathe, hon, breathe," James reminded her. "Breathe and push."

"I can't do both."

"Yes, you can. You're the most amazing woman I know. You can do anything, sweetheart. Anything. Now breathe."

"No," she cried, knowing her body was tearing in half. She could feel it tearing, feel her flesh ripping from her bones—that had to be what was happening down there.

Then there was the pressure.

The intense, almighty pressure that pushed against her insides, demanding she expand, grant passage.

"Lots of dark hair, Melissa." James's voice sounded hoarse, husky. "I see lots of dark hair."

God, she wished she could see.

But that would require opening her eyes, and she'd shut them, squeezed them tight to the blinding pain.

"Breathe, Melissa, breathe," James reminded her again, and she bit back the retort for him to shut up and breathe. "The contraction's coming to an end. One more time. We're almost there."

We nothing. She was doing all the work. He was just sitting there, telling her to breathe. The pain in her body eased enough with the end of her contraction that she opened her eyes to tell him exactly what she thought of his *we*.

Only their eyes met and she forgot to breathe again. This time for a totally different reason. Not from pain, but because of love.

James's eyes worshiped *her*, looked at her with such raw emotion that she suspected any wall he'd ever had had crumbled beyond repair.

Was it because of the baby? Was that why he looked that way? *Had to be.*

She searched his gaze, looking for answers to her heart's questions and afraid to hope, to dream.

"Tell me again, Melissa," he demanded in a hoarse whisper.

"Tell you what?" she asked, feeling the first new twinges of muscles pulling in her back and abdomen, signaling the onset of another contraction.

"That you wish you'd married me."

Fighting the rising tension in her muscles, she did. "I wish I'd come home that night, that you'd been here to give me that ring. I wish you'd never left, because I need you." Her words came out as pants now. "I want to be your wife. Always."

What did it matter what she was telling him? Any moment she was going to die from the pain. It cut so deep she knew there was no way she'd survive. If she was going to die, she wanted James to know the truth.

"More than that," she gasped, focused on pushing downward, using the contraction to make her efforts more effective. Quick pants. Hard pushes. "I want you to be my husband," she panted.

"Melissa."

The raw emotion with which he said her name forced her eyes to open, to stay locked with his.

"I've been yours since the moment we met."

What was he saying?

A huge pressure shot forth, seeming to split her insides, and she cried out.

Oh, God.

"You did good, Sweetheart, but don't push," James ordered, no longer looking at her but working between her legs. "The baby's head's out."

Although she knew he was moving between her legs, she no longer felt anything, just focused on the pressure inside her.

"Beautiful," James murmured, clearing the baby's throat. "Absolutely beautiful. With the next contraction, Melissa. Just one more."

Hadn't he already said that?

But there was no time to think, because the tight band around her stomach yanked again. She dropped back, her spine arching, her body intent on expelling the pressure, on easing her burden.

"James, I can't do this," she cried.

"You can, honey. Just a little more. Give a big push. Now."

She did, feeling a rush of pressure and fluid and like her body had turned inside out.

"You did it, Melissa." His voice choked up. She strained her neck, trying to see.

A startled, unhappy wail burst through Melissa's chest, grabbed her heart, and clenched.

Her eyes met James's shining ones, but only briefly as he continued checking the baby.

"Apgar score is ten." A perfect score. "Meet your daughter." He cradled the still-attached-by-the-umbilical-cord baby in his arms.

Daughter?

Melissa blinked at the tiny, messy bundle in his arms, watched him wrap a clean towel around *her*. She reached out to stroke her finger over a rosy cheek.

"A girl?"

Glancing up from the baby he stared at in awe, he grinned. "All along."

"But…"

James placed the baby in her arms. "You made assumptions without having all the facts."

Melissa stared at the perfect little girl in her arms. Ten fingers. Ten toes. Perfect round face and head with a shock of jet-black hair. Big dark blue eyes like most babies were born with, but Melissa suspected they'd stay blue. Like James's.

A girl.

"I bought boy clothes."

Moving back between her legs to clean her and deliver the afterbirth, he grinned, a mischievous twinkle sparkling in his eyes. "I've got pink covered."

A few minutes later, after James had clamped and cut the cord, Melissa touched a tiny hand, and five fingers automatically grasped hers. "You bought pink?"

James motioned to where the baby attempted to cram her free fist into her mouth. "My trunk is a baby girl's treasure trove. I knew you'd want to have pink to bring her home from the hospital."

"Why didn't you say anything?"

"Because you said you didn't want to know the gender." He wiped his hands on a towel, then clasped her hand, the one the baby held onto, and the image of their three hands bound together brought tears to her eyes.

"I really do attempt to give you what you want, Melissa."

"Then give me you." She averted her gaze to stare at the pink baby, her sweet little lips puckered.

"I told you, you've had me all along."

"Not these past few months. You haven't held me, touched me, not even when I begged you to."

"I wanted you to know sex wasn't what bound us together. That although I want you fiercely, what I feel for you is much more. I wanted you to miss me."

"I did miss you. Horribly." She closed her eyes, then met his gaze. "If you only knew how many nights I lay in bed, wishing you were there to hold me, knowing you were just a few doors down and yet so far away."

"I was never far away, babe." He lifted her hand to his lips, kissed her palm. "I've always been right here, with you."

Hot tears ran down her cheeks. "I thought I'd lost you."

"Those same nights, I was lying in the guest room, wishing you'd come to me, that I had the right to go to you. I couldn't. I wasn't willing to risk you making me leave if I overstepped the mark. Not when I wanted to be here so badly I could have kicked myself for ever leaving. I love you, Melissa. I have from the moment you first took my breath away at that asthma meeting."

She couldn't doubt him. Not with the way he looked at her, with the way his eyes lit with truth.

"You did some breath-stealing of your own at that meeting."

He laced his fingers with hers.

"I love you, too, James. With all my heart and all my soul and all that I am." Her mind raced, wanting to tell him everything in her heart. "I'll move to Nashville, sell my practice, stay home with the baby, work by your side. Whatever it is that'll make you happy, I'll do it. I just want you in my life. That's most important."

He shook his head and gave a small chuckle. "You'd never be happy in Nashville."

"I'll never be happy without you."

"You don't have to be without me."

"You're OK with commuting, with staying here? My working at the clinic and you driving back and forth?"

"It worked for months."

Unable to resist, she ran her fingertip over the baby's cheek. "But not with you being happy."

"I wasn't happy because I didn't know how you felt, because we were growing apart. Because we hadn't been honest with each other. You on how much you wanted a family, me on the reasons why I didn't."

"Cailee's death wasn't your fault," she quickly assured him.

Glancing at the sleeping baby in her arms, he nodded. "If I could do it over, I'd hold Cailee every moment of that night, but I can't relive the past. I can only make sure I don't repeat the same mistakes in the future. Luckily, we know much more about the causes and prevention of SIDS than we did seventeen years ago. I know that." He touched her cheek. "But I have decided to give up my job at the ER."

She gasped. "You can't do that."

"I wasn't going to tell you for a while but…" he shrugged "…I already have."

"I thought you were just on leave."

"Last week they needed to know if I planned to come back and I told them that I was going to do whatever it took to be with you, the mother of my child and the owner of my heart."

"James, you're not planning to stand twenty-four-hour-a-day vigil over me and the baby, are you?"

He smiled softly and shook his head. "I just want to be closer, to be able to be here when you and the baby need me. You're both too precious for me to be away, working all the time."

She digested what he was saying. "But your teaching? Your research?"

"I enjoy what I do, but if it's necessary to make things work, I'll give them up, too."

Melissa repositioned the warm bundle in her arms. "You'd do that for me?"

"In a heartbeat."

"James, I was wrong. So wrong about so many things. I should have talked to you about how I felt rather than throwing myself into my work. It's just what I've always done, how I've dealt with things beyond my control. But I don't need my work. I need you and our baby. You don't have to give up anything in Nashville. I could be happy anywhere in the world so long as you're by my side."

"That would be Sawtooth, Tennessee, because I've become quite attached to Caren Little and her sleeping disorder," he teased.

Melissa frowned, wondering what he was talking about and why he'd bring a patient up at a time like this. She also wondered how she could have ever not known where her heart belonged when it thudded so hard just for him.

"James, what am I going to do with all those little-boy clothes?"

"Save them for next time."

"Next time?"

"You do want more than one, right?" His eyes searched hers. "Because I predict you're going to contract Mrs Little's sleeping disorder in about a month."

"A month?"

Smiling wickedly, he nodded. A month. Melissa blushed. About the time her body would allow her to become sexually active again.

"Marry me, Melissa. Make me whole, have my babies, and spend your life letting me love you and our children."

Her vision blurring with tears, happy tears, she nodded.

Far away in the distance, they heard the wail of the ambulance. Soon they would be on their way to Dekalb.

"We're going to make this work, aren't we?" she asked, a smile playing on her lips because in her heart there was no need to ask. She knew the answer. It shone brightly in James's eyes when he looked at her and their daughter.

"Oh, yeah, Dr Conner." He leaned forward, kissed

her squarely on the mouth. "We're going to work out beautifully. This time we have love on our side, and that's a surefire prescription for a happy ending."

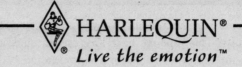

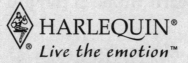

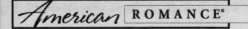
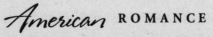
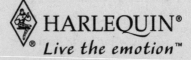

HARLEQUIN®
INTRIGUE®

BREATHTAKING ROMANTIC SUSPENSE

Shared dangers and passions lead to electrifying romance and heart-stopping suspense!

Every month, you'll meet six new heroes who are guaranteed to make your spine tingle and your pulse pound. With them you'll enter into the exciting world of Harlequin Intrigue— where your life is on the line and so is your heart!

THAT'S INTRIGUE— ROMANTIC SUSPENSE AT ITS BEST!

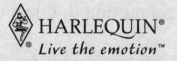

HARLEQUIN®
Live the emotion™

www.eHarlequin.com   INTDIR06

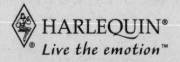